MECHAGNOSIS

BY
DOUGLAS THOMPSON

Published by
Dog Horn Publishing
45 Monk Ings, Birstall, Batley WF17 9HU
United Kingdom
doghornpublishing.com
sales@doghornpublishing.com

Cover and interior art by
Douglas Thompson,
based on reconstructions of the
Antikythera mechanism, 1st Century BC

Chapter One first appeared in *Polluto 7* (Autumn, 2010), under the title 'Mechagnosis'.

UK Distribution: Central Books
99 Wallis Road, London, E9 5LN, United Kingdom
orders@centralbooks.com
Phone:+44 (0) 845 458 9911
Fax: +44 (0) 845 458 9912

Overseas (Non-UK) Distribution: Lulu Press, Inc
3101 Hillsborough Street
Raleigh, NC 27607
Phone # +1 919 459 5858
Fax # +1 919 459 5867
purchaseorder@lulu.com

ACKNOWLEDGEMENTS

Thanks to: Nina Allan, Andrew Hook, Victoria Hooper, Adam Lowe, Rona MacDonald, David Rix, Stephen Theaker, and Steve Upham.

The translations from Rilke's *Duino Elegies* are based on those by David Young, published by W. W. Norton & Company, 1978.

ALSO BY DOUGLAS THOMPSON

Ultrameta
Sylvow
Apoidea
Entanglement

MECHAGNOSIS contents

MECHAGNOSIS #01

~The Machine Starts~

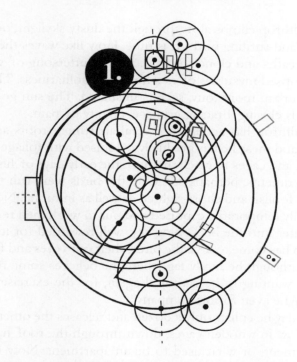

"If I cried out who would hear me up there among the angelic orders? And suppose one suddenly took me to his heart I would shrivel, I couldn't survive next to his greater existence. Beauty is only the first touch of terror we can still bear, and it awes us so much because it so coolly disdains to destroy us . . . "
—Rainer Maria Rilke, from the *Duino Elegies*, #1.

Scott Malthrop climbs aloft through the dusty skylight, out to the big roof and ruffling birds. It is time. How like waves their wings lift his breaths and cloud the eyes. Fresh fluttersong of washing-lines: glimpsed mysteries of neighbours in solitariness. The sweet grain of urban monotony, secrets unshared. The sun goes down like eyelids closing, bracing grimace, dignity of pain.

Malthrop has access to several apartment roofs as well as his own, and these he has gradually colonised with foliage and bait for birds, and cages to catch them. In the early days of his father's first experiments, perhaps some of the birds were run to death. This was foolish and short-sighted as well as immoral. Now every bird is only temporarily captured and put to work then re-released a week later into the beckoning sky, well-rewarded for its labour. Malthrop has come to love the birds, their calm eyes and fluttering hearts. Although he rarely tags them, he believes some return on purpose, wanting to be captured again, for the exercise and the food, maybe even for his company.

Today he enlists only a dozen and releases the others, taking them below in wooden cages, down through the roof hatch into his apartment, or what used to be an apartment. Now it is only residual, marginal, left over space around *The Machine*. The Machine occupies all three storeys of his narrow urban townhouse, from front to back, cogs and levers up against windows and walls, floor joists long cut away and braced to make room for wheels and pistons.

He times his start-up phase to coincide with the busiest periods of traffic outside, so the neighbours will not be overly alarmed by the considerable vibrations. Sometimes he likes to use a few seagulls for extra power, but today the team are all pigeons, city doves, his trusty stalwarts. The Intake Platforms consist of wheels and wing harnesses within ventilated glass tanks and seed dispensers. Malthrop kisses and caresses each bird one after the other, calming and soothing its palpitations before depositing it

8

gently down a one-way tube onto its running wheel. When all twelve avian pilots are assembled, he salutes them with a tired smile then descends below to rope himself into the control room.

We say "control", and yet the whole essence of this room is a lack of control. A statistical degree of hazard has been built in, essential to guarantee a sense of danger on the part of the operator. A one in one hundred chance always exists that the Dead Man's Lever will fall and Malthrop suffocate in sand or water. In such a scenario, his skeleton will eventually become part of The Machine, as his father and mother are already: just one of a thousand sentimental objects incorporated for esoteric functions which somehow contribute to its overall spiritual charge.

One thing is for certain: when The Machine is working, every component, at some point, must move. The toy yacht with white sails that his father built him when he was aged three, will rotate and rock on salty waves in an old bathtub. His mother's swimsuit will be stretched and flexed like a washing machine's drive-band. The crackling gramophone record of the sound of seagulls will repeat while the sand from the first beach he ever played on pours like an hourglass from vessel to vessel: colourful bright plastic pales from beaches; grim janitorial buckets that caught waterdrops from the roof leaks in his first school.

Malthrop sits and writes his diary entry, aware as ever that it may be his last:

The word "Nostalgia" was only invented in 1688, by the Swiss physician Johannes Hofer, to describe a medical condition of near-fatal homesickness. If, as Wittgenstein said, "the limits of my language mean the limits of my world", then did nostalgia simply not exist before this date, if it could only be so clumsily denoted as wistfulness for days passed?

Father made me memorise the dates. 1674: The English agricultural pioneer Jethro Tull is born. 1701: he invents the seed drill, setting off the Agricultural Revolution and in turn the Industrial Revolution. Mechanisation gets underway and the traditional way of life of the rural peasant is doomed to history. This is how history works: from the tiniest insignificance a chain of events grows too slowly for anyone to ponder or stop. A seed drill is invented and men land on the moon. The Machine starts. Tonight I might die.

—Scott Malthrop, son of Scott Malthrop Senior (deceased), 30th April 2020.

9

Malthrop binds and gags himself until completely helpless, throws his head back onto The Starter Pad. The chamber he is locked within begins to fall and rotate on an infinitesimally slow orbit through The Presses. Although, like life on Earth, at any given moment he can feel entirely static, in truth he is perpetually in motion and danger. Gradually over hours, water and soil come and go: plants from his parents' garden, grass from the park where he kissed his first girlfriend, water from the bath in which he drowned her. His wrist bindings are coils of her black hair, and when The Machine stretches him over its cruellest segments, deprived of air, he will struggle and her tresses will dig deep into his flesh as he screams, washed in his own blood and tears.

Above him or below somewhere, as the great calibrated wheels rotate, the birds will flap and pedal on with industrial ferocity, rest-times kicking in and alternating, the tag team dutifully working through the night. Their calm eyes remain relentless in their purpose, profoundly understood. Animals have no concept of futility.

What was the first machine in the world I wonder? The slingshot? The Shadoof? Archimedes' Screw? The Buddhist prayer wheel . . . now there's an interesting one: a machine played by the wind, by the Gods themselves, with only a spiritual purpose. Sometime after the dawn of the machine age, the backlash quietly began: the absurd machines of eccentric inventors have sprung up simultaneously all over the planet, like spring flowers magically blossoming in the shade of a broad oak. Heath Robinson, Rube Goldberg, *every culture today has its own name and equivalent: in France* The Gas Factory, *Denmark* Storm P Machines, *in Bengal* Abol Tool, *in Japan* Chindōgu *and* Pythagoras Switch, *Turkey* Zihni Sinir Proceleri. *The beauty and universal appeal of these devices, particularly to children (the most devout little anarchists amongst us), resides in their very inefficiency, their transparent futility. But Man and Machine have unfinished business since 1701. Has irrational beauty really no term within our mathematical equations? If these machines are pointless then Life is pointless. But if we can bring ourselves to say that such machines are sublimely beautiful, what then? Then the metaphor, the microcosm is grasped, and we may be healed. The most perfectly futile, the most sublime and absurd machines of all are of*

*course: ourselves. We must embrace futility and absurdity. We must seize the
machines that so wound us and make them part of us again, make love to
them, make them as magnificently ludicrous as ourselves. Then we, and they,
will be whole again, and God will smile.*

Malthrop's mother had been obsessed with cleanliness. The
droning of the vacuum cleaner not once but twice a week, was
the oppressive music of his childhood. Not satisfied with this, she
had purchased a separate vacuum for each storey of the house
and inducted Malthrop and his father into operating each of
these simultaneously while she worked her fastidious routine. The
resultant wall of noise must have tried the neighbours' patience
sorely, but since Malthrop seldom saw them he soon presumed
them stone deaf, mad, or dead from the attrition. Perhaps they
were good solid walls, and just as well.

What drove his father most to despair, was how the
Hoovering regime had to go on regardless of other commitments
and weather. Although Malthrop's parents were fond of a
weekend walk together in the country, often this would have to
be undertaken at sunset, twilight, or black of night, the day's
preceding sunlight having been cruelly squandered on the manic
removal of dust.

Then there were the washing machines. Three of them. One
each. Malthrop believed that other families allowed their worn
linen to accumulate for a day or two, in charming wicker baskets.
But in his mother's regime anything handed in dirty would have to
be washed within the hour, even if it meant it had to be the only
item in the drum. It was inconceivable to him how he might go
about explaining to his school teachers that he was exhausted and
inattentive in class due to sleep loss from washing machine noise.
He almost envied his classmates their simpler traditional pleasures
of fighting parents and teenage brothers with loud music.

When The Machine is in perfect motion: whirring, exquisitely
organised, and Malthrop bound, robbed of control of his own
destiny; he can at last begin to dream and drift. Time dissolves

11

for hours and days on end. He has no moon or sunlight, partial sensory deprivation takes hold. Space, the materiality of the walls, dissolves. He sees a beach, perhaps it is the sand pouring down tubes near his neck, but no: he is really there now on that beach. He stands up and looks around. He looks down and sees his arms are bound with seaweed, breaking off easily, dissolving. He feels a rumbling beneath his feet, and kneels down and brushes some sand away: he realises the entire Machine is still working, but buried under the sand. He laughs to himself and walks across the top of it and on towards a strange apparition: a hedge maze, here on the edge of the sea. Where is this? Does he remember this place at all?

He first met Melanie in the summer pavilion in the Botanic Gardens. Summer rain had forced them both indoors, total strangers, running from different directions towards each other, closing the flimsy wooden doors behind them like a conspiracy. Her long hair soaked with rain was like a static waterfall, a gleaming black fountain of life. Her eyes, breaking into laughter as sunlight re-emergent: struck the dewdrops like bells, sparkling diadems on spiders webs at the trellised eaves.

She had asked him the time of day and he had shrugged and pointed calmly to her watch. *Oh, this? It's stopped, I'm afraid.* Her long slender arm bore something gold and Swiss.

May I? She shivered sweetly as he took her wrist. *I am a jeweller, I might . . .* Her eyes widened as he took it apart in front of her, too stunned to stop him until the peril was over before it had begun, the piece returned to her in good order. *I think you'll find it will work now . . .* he smiled modestly.

You make jewellery, watches?—she marvelled.

Repair other people's mostly, he sighed, gazing out again at the bleak rain, *-but occasionally I get to work on something new.*

How did you learn?

From my father.

A family business?

Well, it is mine now, the work ruined his hands and eyes, as it may do mine, in time . . .

But you have such lovely hands, she gasped, surprised at herself for being so forward, *the fingers . . .*

Long and sensitive, like a girls?—he blushed, old playground taunts echoing through his inner ear.

Like an artist . . . she said smiling, and closed his hand around itself like a flower.

The importance of words again. Even the word "Luddite" has been carefully sabotaged and barbed by modern historians and sociologists, to police the minds of the present generation. The Luddites did not oppose machines or destroy machines out of wanton hatred. They left intact the mills and weaving machines of anyone who had not used the increased productivity to lower their prices and wages. They were opposed in other words, not to machines, but to an economic system that used machines to make ordinary people's lives worse, not better. Their simple question was one that should still be asked today about every new invention before we embrace it, but never is: will it improve our experience of life? -Enhance or diminish our sense of our selves? Do we actually need it?

This was no trivial matter. It was the British Empire's equivalent of Rome's Spartacus and the Slave Revolt. At times in 1813, more soldiers were fighting Luddite armies than were fighting Napolean's forces in Spain. Thousands of Luddites were tried and deported and imprisoned for life. "Machine Breaking" was made a capital crime. Ring leaders were hung and beheaded in public. Right from the start, machines have been a serious business.

Malthrop's mother. Dust to dust. Dust was, and is, everywhere. Not like stains and spills with someone to blame and the hope of avoidance. Dust happens. The fear of dust is like the rejection of time and life itself. To clean it away is to say you wish to die, to cancel out your own sordid stain upon eternity. To Malthrop, his mother always seemed to live life as a dress rehearsal, a dance alone on a blank stage she had to keep clean until something better happened. But nothing happens if the stage is kept blank. *Please Mrs Malthrop, can Scott Junior come out to play?*—his friend Vince's disappointed face at the door. Bringing friends back would, of

13

course, increase the likelihood of mess and stains, so better not to have them. Life, in short, is horribly likely to incur death. So don't live. Clean. Constantly.

There was an accident in the end. Stairs are fiercely hard to keep clean, the most wear-and-tear combined with the most awkward angles. Something fell or twisted, a Hoover dropped through space into a stairwell like a plunging pendulum and his mother was strangulated, her limbs pinned through a balustrade. Whatever cries she may have emitted were of course, entirely inaudible to her dutifully employed spouse and issue, engaged in their own sonic blitzkriegs on separate floors. For years afterwards, Malthrop found his frozen memory of the scene of her demise he chanced upon, impossible to consider as anything other than a grotesque art installation.

A good deal of The Machine having been built by his father, Malthrop can never be entirely certain of its next move. Is it the third day now, or the fourth? He has totally lost track of time. The adapted railway track has gradually taken him towards the basement and the Chamber of Slicing Mirrors, lined with his grandmother's fur coats, the intoxicating aroma of mink and fox and mothballs and old mould. The mirrors flood slowly with boiling hot water this time, and various childhood trinkets: rubber ducks and toys come bobbing down to meet him, the inane grin on a clown face mocking him in frozen caricature of sadistic mirth as the vicious steam accumulates.

Suddenly a further door opens and an autumnal bonfire scaulds him, piles of leaves blow over him, black embers sting his eyes. Damp grass and earth are everywhere: he is helping his father chop wood as a child. He can smell his dad's tweed jacket, the rubber of his boots. He is back in time. His parents have just had a fight, and Malthrop's mother has stormed off threatening never to return, but they know she will, like all the other times. There is a quiet camaraderie brewing between father and son, like a teapot on the hob, like a bonfire gone past its peak and safe to leave unattended. Smiling, late, coldish sunlight is in his father's eyes, the glint of wisdom in his spectacles, the sweat on his brow:

the fruit of honest toil rather than nervous tension, for a change. Things will be alright. Malthrop wants to stay there forever: with the smell of sacks of fresh-fallen apples laid out on the kitchen floor.

If only the world had made it easier to report Mother's death. The forms, the certificates, the weeks and months of insensitive bureaucracy, the disbelief from every faceless organisation, forcing my father to photocopy her death certificate over and over again and take it like a naughty schoolboy with a punishment exercise to show his bank manager, just to get access to their joint account. A hundred phonecalls from a hundred companies demanding that the flagrant charade of fraudulent death be admitted to. After the many indignities that this society heaps on every individual throughout their life, it saves its best one until last: that even to die is some kind of transgression, a non-sequitur in the capitalist system, something our relatives are made to feel to blame for, if we are let away with it at all. No, my father and I would sit down together at the end of yet another day of "formalities" and laugh through our tears and grief: how much easier and simpler it would be not to die at all. Indeed, it seems to be what "they" expect of us.

People wonder why great civilisations like the Maya collapsed without apparent reason in the past: and I suspect that one day they will find out the answer is that they invented the application form, then lost the taste for life. Drowned under the weight of their own bureaucracy. Life is too complex to map and categorise. It just happens. But when you try to categorise and file it, it does not.

That was the seed of some of our genius, you see. We resolved there and then that my father would not be buried when the time came, and that our shared names were a great opportunity. So I am officially a hundred and sixty years old now and have the longest running state pension in recorded history. Except history isn't recording me.

Melanie was always trying to keep fit. Malthrop went with her a few times to the local gymnasium and was always horrified by the machines they had there. There was something vile and intermittent in their motion. They had no fluidity of purpose, no holistic integration. Running machines, walking machines: then why had Melanie driven them both to the gym? She was never able to answer this, as if it was a ludicrous question that only a simpleton would ask. Why simulate a three mile walk when you could just take one? And those weights and devices for stretching pectoral and biceps, the forces they exerted seemed horribly oblique, unfamiliar, the aches and pains they left you with like the aftermath of some grossly unnatural act that you might want to confess to a doctor or priest.

The scene in the gym amazed Malthrop: of rank after rank of running youths confined like battery hens, counteracting their mental boredom with video and audio through wires and screens. It seemed like distilled futility, stripped of its customary clothes, as if your employer were to ask you to lick every stamp you would ever need in your life in just one afternoon, or make every cup of coffee you'd need for a year in advance.

Melanie was young, her figure was perfect, but God had made it that way, not gymnasiums, and not Melanie herself. It had always struck Malthrop as ludicrous how a woman might thank you if you praised her good looks, as if she could have been in any way eligible for credit for her own physical creation. Praising her parents might make more sense, but even then it would only be for not having damaged her. Insane though it sounds, and Malthrop was by no means religious, praising a woman for her looks had always struck him as something close to blasphemy.

Malthrop is sitting in a bar in the Canal District, telling his old school friend Vince about the early days of The Machine, after his mother died. His father had gone quite strange for a while, and thought about starting his own religion. He had set out to find some followers. Vince laughs as Malthrop tells him how when he was just thirteen he had been made to take a collection box around the dusty old wooden pews of a derelict church, looking with doe-eyes for donations from gatherings of various social outcasts, semi down-and-outs, and mental cases. The Machine was much smaller then, a less advanced prototype only the size of one room, and a few privileged believers who came visiting were allowed access to the Mechanised Revelation of Sublime

Absurdity, a private view.

Malthrop can still remember fragments of his father's sermons:

The Industrial Age has robbed much of the Human race of its dignity, remade us all in its own image. It seems as if to be a good citizen we must do our very best to resemble robots. Mankind has redefined itself in terms of the machine, even in our very language to describe ourselves: upgrades, products, consumers, dysfunctional, social services, integration, productivity. But the opposite process is still possible and necessary. Humanise the machines, make them artistic and restless and pointless, vain and unreasonable, contrary and vicious, capricious and scandalously beautiful, just as we are. Fuck the machines before they fuck you!

But he can't have said that in a church! Vince objects loudly, standing up and slamming his glass on the table, *-and why would you risk telling me this?* Malthrop looks up to see that the left side of Vince's face is melting as if it is a billposter soaked in rain, and one of his hands is turning gleaming silver. Malthrop steps away from the table and Vince's hand has become an egg-whisker now, a whirring liquidiser that he is lifting threateningly towards his face, as his voice turns into Malthrop's mother's, harping on about cleanliness and godliness.

Something's wrong, the electric bulb overhead blinks and Malthrop knocks Vince aside and staggers over to the far wall, holding his temples, a throbbing headache taking hold. He draws the tall black curtains to the function room aside and instead of the expected amplifiers and beer kegs he finds The Machine humming and whirring and turning, its dials flashing, shaking the floor. He turns back and sees the room is fading, Vince has curled up under the table and is whimpering as he turns into a pet dog.

Malthrop is back in The Machine. Can it be day five? He has soiled himself and the pain and fatigue are growing unbearable, his leg bindings cutting through the skin. Multi-coloured electric wires are visible around him now: the Zone Of Memories Of Lightning perhaps, or of Every Computer You Have Ever Worked On. The meditations crush him. Every drawing and document he has ever done seen from the perspective of each hard drive and processor. The slow passage of dull days encoded in binary, the flashing of electrons. Like looking at yourself as a fourteen mile

17

high statue from the perspective of a flea on your shoe. Time, molecular time. Only during sensory deprivation can you grasp the horror of each infinite instant.

A switch clicks and the first of a series of agonising electric shocks convulses Malthrop in the comfortless darkness. A surprise: something nice his father left him.

Of course he had tried to delay for as long as possible Melanie gaining entry to the house. Stories of his father being a dangerous drunkard, a madman, incontinent, the house unsanitary, apt to run around naked. These had held her at bay for a whole three months, no small achievement, until that day . . .

Melanie had opened the double doors from the cramped kitchenette, expecting as any normal human being would, to clap eyes upon a living room, a fireplace, perhaps an elderly father sitting beside it with a rug on his knees. The shock and the scream were horribly immediate. The problem was one of distance, focal depth denied to the expectant eye. There in front of her and stretching high above as she staggered back in disbelief: was a wall of blackened machinery, hideously complex, engraved, crenellated, cogged, annotated, and calibrated with numerals and symbols mathematical and alchemical. She turned to the other doors, to other cupboards, unmasking the demon, uncovering the precarious status of her own existence: a lie of a room, a mere charade, a paper-thin stage set over the gates of Hell, a Sunday hat upon a putrefying corpse. This small room was all that was left of the house, and the scene within it doomed.

She wept as he tried to embrace her, he gripped her as she turned away. *Do you even have a father?!*

He's in there . . . he muttered weakly and she knew with a killing certainty that he didn't mean alive. Her struggling wounded then angered him. If she had calmly reflected and discussed, then she might have walked away. Then things would have been different. But her screams and his despair at her failure to understand, her kicks and his lunges became the same motion, a composite machine, an opposite of sex, a fight. An immortality of sorts for her, no more need to breathe for him, the ultimate

18

mortician. The bones, the sinews, the hair, the teeth all retain the deeper beauty. All else is betrayed by time, better burned away.

Another twist in the machine: the sound of huge Victorian trees filled with roaring winds, memories of spring walks by the reservoir: the great grass ramparts to roll down, built a century before by Irish navvies. Flying a kite with his father, a small dog running after it like repelling an aerial invasion. A dark clay casserole pot on the stove upon their shivering return: orange of chopped carrots, dust of flour on tables, his mother's mohair jumper the pale powder blue of April skies. Relatives that didn't come today. School jotters, Sunday stomach, exercises to be done, the clean perfection of baths and mathematics.

Malthrop walks through the hedge maze by the seaside under the perfect sun and is not as surprised as he ought to be to see the figure of Melanie dressed in period costume, twirling a white parasol over her head, as he breaks into a run to meet her.

Mel . . . he begins, but as she slowly turns he sees her face has become a clock, with Roman numerals and fine brass hands approaching noon.

The wind howls and blows sand across the paths of the maze and Malthrop is suddenly overcome with a sense of profound tiredness and loneliness. There seems something glassy and wistful in the deep blue of the distant waves, like some forgotten afternoon from childhood, pregnant with dim expectation. *What happened, Melanie, can you still speak?*

Time happens . . . a voice says, but Malthrop turns to see the words come from his father seated on a park bench nearby, in the form of a white skeleton wearing a black suit, his head in his hands, as if in despair.

Now Melanie has drifted closer, and as the brass hands strike the hour, a little door opens where her mouth should be, and a cuckoo flies out. Malthrop turns and runs after it, anxious to find The Machine again under the sand, not to remain trapped in this world. *We are all contraptions* . . . the bird sings incessantly in his ear as he moves through the dune grasses, *-but who will repair us?*

He is relieved as he nears the beach again and feels the deep hum of The Machine under his toes.

The Machine slows at last and Malthrop wakes: a thin spray of cold water is falling over his forehead, as his foot shackles are released by a timeswitch, the control room door springing open.

Freedom again, for another week or so perhaps. Like all the monks and nuns in seclusion the world over, Malthrop knows that without his sacrifice, his peculiar form of prayer to worship the Machine Age, everything out there would fall apart. Civilisation would finally entirely disintegrate into chaos and damnation without the slightest inkling as to where the body-blow had come from.

Malthrop walks through the marginal zones, the dark leftover gangways of his house, steam pouring off him and from the open door of The Machine behind him. He keeps his eyes aloft as he climbs ladders and narrow wooden stairs, fragments of sky and sunlight flickering from above, drawing him on. He is streaked with blood and sweat, sand and soil, his own urine and faeces. But before he showers he goes to the platforms and releases the doves, gathering some of them up in his arms and on his shoulders as he staggers the last stair flight and bursts out onto the rooftop, rejoicing beneath the vast blue sky. The birds flutter and cluck and twitter, sharing his joy.

How many years has he lived like this? Alone, but enshrined, adorned, tormented and exalted by the museum of his own memories, the machine of his consciousness? He goes to the parapet edge and looks out across the many roofs and gardens, the roads and rails, the patchwork quilt of lives. None of them know of his Machine, they remain ignorant of how it keeps their world in balance, regulating, rejuvenating it. Beneath their million roofs they can know nothing of him and yet, somehow, this morning at least, he feels he can know each of them. How can it be? He feels that no mind, no life, is beyond him. He can travel through all walls, physical and temporal, no door is locked. He raises a hand as if in regal blessing to the scene below, and a dove comes and lands fluttering on his fingers, interrogating him with its calm and deathless gaze, and he laughs, nobody to witness the miracle.

MECHAGNOSIS #02

~ *Angels, it seems* ~

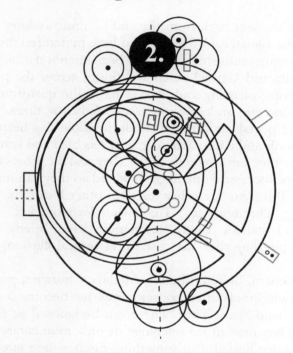

"*But the living are wrong in the sharp distinctions they make. Angels, it seems, don't always know if they're moving among the living or the dead. The drift of eternity drags all the ages of man through both of those spheres and its sound rises over them both . . .*"
—Rainer Maria Rilke, from the *Duino Elegies*, #1.

Two angels are sent back from the end of time, looking for traces, openings, the signatures of those who have punctured the temporal fabric. Sometimes these breaches have been intentional, as at Geneva: where Seralta and Merkiel perch and flutter across the picturesque Swiss rooftops, puzzling and marvelling at the quantum wreckage strewn around the underground racetrack below them. Burnt-out filaments of portals and time-wounds, invisible slag-heaps of fried particles, pools and eddies where gravity has bled and scabbed over.

These they can attend to easily. They seal the errors over, clean up, the more successful openings stabilised so they can make use of them later. But there are other traces in other locations. Tunguska, Teutoburg, Thermopylae, Treblinka. Experiments, accidents, anomalies. Instances where terrestrials have briefly witnessed something puzzling then dismissed it as optical illusion, a trick of the mind.

Bethlehem, Belsen. Munich, Medina. Churches, great battles, massacres: whirlpools where consciousness has become concentrated enough to bend Space-Time. These can be ignored or ring-fenced generally. They present no openings or only momentary ones that have long since healed. But something catches their attention, and Seralta and Merkiel fly north over the sea to London.

There, the house of Scott Malthrop Junior has already been encased in a concrete sarcophagus, for all the world like a tiny urban Chernobyl. Scarcely anyone recalls anymore that this structure is even here, so many centuries of building and rebuilding having gone on around it. It appears dead and inert to the few casual human eyes who notice it, but the angels see it differently.

At this moment the city is frozen, in time as well as winter. To Seralta and Merkiel, every snow flake hovers in mid-air, and every person going about their business that evening is similarly halted, mouths open, hands raised, legs running or static as befits each case, thus entirely unaware of the angels who move unseen among them: too quick for their eyes, fast as flickering butterflies.

24

So now above the light-streams of traffic Seralta kneels on a neighbouring roof and peers through the concrete into the dim inner core of the entombed house. *What do you see?*—Merkiel asks, taking a few snow flakes off the air onto his tongue, then flying down to her side, his transparent skin flickering briefly to reveal blue flames and a maze of red veins like organic circuitry.

You're curious then? You want to attempt this? Seralta asks, kneeling to scratch the tiny white wings at her ankles, sighing, drinking in the cool night air and glancing up at him and the innumerable stars over his shoulder.

Merkiel alights onto the thin layer of snow on the sarcophagus roof, and emits a beam of light from his left eye which begins to slowly bore down towards the centre of the strange tomb below him, seeking out the dim outline of a figure he can make out there, burrowing a route towards this mysterious pharaoh.

Malthrop wakes and knows he has missed something. The memory of Melanie surrounds him in his cramped mattress suspended on a clothes pulley from the kitchen ceiling. He lets himself down then washes at the sink. Eats a breakfast of corned beef straight from the tin, takes a photograph of Melanie from the drawer and examines it closely for fifteen minutes.

He looks in the fridge. It is dismayingly empty, he needs to go out. It is nearing nightfall again, the only time he allows himself to go out anymore. He dresses in loose baggy jeans and jacket, T-shirt underneath, then jogs out into the night, looking carefully in every direction before locking the door.

In a nearby market, he wanders between stalls, picking up fruit, milk, a few cuts of meat. From the corner of his eye: a blurred distant face beyond two stalls stiffens and darts, focussing, its mouth opens, a voice calls out: *Hey, Scott!*

Malthrop hurls his groceries into his haversack and ducks into a small crowd, sidetracks down an alleyway. A baker, or chef, in a white smock and hat is reversing out of a narrow doorway in the lane, carrying a large tray of hot rolls. Malthrop starts to dive around him then sees he can't make it and tries to go under the tray, but the assistant emerging from the doorway seems startled and drops the tray, crying out. It falls on Malthrop and he writhes beneath the commotion, cursed then kicked.

Scott? Is that you? Are you ok? Were you running from someone?

M-Mitch! Sorry! I thought you were someone else, I seem to have got in a fankle here.

Do you know this clown?—the chef asks, bared arms, rippling tattoos, a vein in his neck pulsing in anger.

Mitch hands Malthrop a cup of steaming tea in his kitchen. Malthrop feels weird to be back in such a familiar setting, but subtly changed, transfigured by grief and loss.

Man, I've been looking for you. I never knew where you lived, and I couldn't find any address amongst Mel's things. Was that market near your house? Is that your neighbourhood?

Not really . . . Malthrop mumbles, running his hands through his hair. *Mitch, I've been lost since she disappeared, in a dark place, falling* . . .

Tell me about it. You could have called me, you should call me in future. It's a cliché, but it does help to talk.

But does it? It won't bring her back.

Mitch sits down and puts his hand on Malthrop's shoulder. *No. But we can keep her memory alive, can't we? Reflect on who she was, on what she would have wanted of us, how we should live now, what we should each do with our lives next* . . .

Malthrop stares bleakly into the silence until only the ticking of the clock and the humming of the fridge mark the relentless beat of time. *Have you kept her things, Mitch?*

Sure. Her books, clothes, wardrobe, most stuff. I don't know why but I can't think how to part with it. My counsellor says that's normal.

Counselling?

It's helpful . . . *maybe, Scott. Better than nothing, anyway, worth a try. I can give them your details if you like* . . . *hey, didn't the police ever* . . .

The phone rings and they both suddenly jump, and Malthrop is reminded of something for a moment, but can't think what.

As Mitch stands in the hallway, looking towards the frosted glass of the front door, Malthrop moves behind him at the kitchen entrance, but feels irrevocably drawn, enticed towards the door to the bedroom. Shaking, sweating, he keeps his eye on Mitch, but edges down the corridor, noiselessly turning the bedroom door handle, opening the door, and slipping inside.

Not now . . . Mitch is saying. *Something has come up . . . I can't talk.*

Malthrop is quickly immersed in Melanie's clothes, raking through them frantically, stuffing every third or fourth item into his rucksack until he hears Mitch's phone conversation unexpectedly finish.

Scott? Are you in there man? Why's the door jammed? You're freaking me out now, open up!

Malthrop opens the window and climbs up and out onto the neighbouring roofs. The door swells and shakes behind him under the force of Mitch's first push as Malthrop runs from gutter to ridge, scrambling over chimney pots, looking for the street's end. Grey early morning. Low fog drifts across the roofscape, as if Malthrop is running through clouds. The traffic sounds from the street below are strangely muffled.

At the furthest block, he takes a handkerchief from his pocket and ties it over the neighbourhood CCTV before he slides down the drainpipe.

He runs over to the tube station with his hood up. On the Bakerloo Line, he changes direction twice, then in a dead-end tunnel jumps a barricade and ditches his coat and bag in a darkened pile of rubble and re-emerges under the next set of cameras with only a T-shirt and 2 polythene bags, his head exposed but face to the floor.

Descending towards Malthrop through the hole they have bored through sixteen feet of concrete, the angels suddenly experience unexpected turbulence. *What's happening?*—Seralta cries out.

Quantum parameters shifting . . . —Merkiel exclaims before they both collapse onto the floor around the inner chamber in which they can see Malthrop enclosed, strapped into his semi-transparent cockpit, hemmed in by turning pistons and wheels.

Before they can reach forward to touch this scene, Malthrop

and the cockpit dematerialise before their eyes, leaving only the surrounding walls, and these in turn slowly melt to reveal a different location:

. . . A summer room, pale evening window, two figures talking in the gathering dusk, girl and boy. Leaf-shadows from the trees outside bounce and flicker over the walls and the face of the girl, stirred by a cool breeze, the first after a day of damp heat. A fly enters through the window and bounces off the wall. The boy stands at the door, has just entered the room, is talking, although she doesn't seem to want to hear.

Ylneddus gnileef egnarts a evah I . . . —the boy is saying. *Llihc neddus a, moor siht ni gnorw gnihtemos si ereht? Noitinomerp a ekil? Ti leef uoy t'nac.*

The girl shivers. A dog barks outside three times, then whines. Seralta and Merkiel snake around the room invisibly, out of phase, one wrapping around the lampshade like mist, the other unwinding on the floor like a Persian rug, pattern dazzling, dappled, changing in the evening light. *Can they see us?*—Seralta whispers like a wind in the curtains, and Merkiel replies with a shake of his head like a groan in the floorboards. The boy walks closer.

Did you hear me? The boy's voice grows faint and flickers. *I don't think you should go out. I think maybe you are in some kind of danger. This guy . . . I don't like the look of him much.*

You don't? The girl scowls, angry, indignant. *And what are you? Gay? My chaperone?*

Uoy rof tuo eye na peek ot, deid eh erofeb dad desimorp I wonk uoy . . . lem.

Efil elohw ym rof? Hctim, dne siht lliw nehw? Retsis ruoy fo ytnarraw dednetxe siht?

The room flickers, the ceiling shakes and Malthrop explodes through the walls, tied to his cradle and cockpit, goggles on, huge metal wheels and pistons cutting through the floor.

What's happening?—Seralta shouts aloud. The girl dissolves as Merkiel reaches out to touch her and flames run down his arms and the curtains catch fire. The room is suddenly filled with storm-force winds. The floor turns into a turbulent ocean criss-crossed by waves on which the boy somehow remains standing,

28

while Seralta and Merkiel both fall into the water, grappling with splintered planks and chairs to stay afloat. The wind roars and waves lash the walls. The wheel turns with Malthrop at its apex, lurching forward, then plunges into the waves as the window shatters inwards, each shard hitting and shredding and dissolving the boy into fragments of light as he falls over.

On the Northern Line, Malthrop notices some Korean students playing with their mobile phones, iPods, Xboxes and laptops. They seem hypnotised, their eyes lit up by the eerie green and blue light from their screens. It occurs to him that they are in some sort of religious ecstasy, their body and soul given over to someone else: the programmer or corporation who has contrived to so utterly entertain them and relieve them of their money. One of them looks up to check what station they're approaching and they pack up in an instant, hoisting their rucksacks, pilgrims setting out for their next station of the Cross. King's Cross.

Their uniformly black hair and smooth features remind him of statues or wax candles, and as he walks behind them through the labyrinth of connecting brick vaulted tunnels he thinks of a city of catacombs where the light of day is never seen and its perfect inhabitants walk blindly, centralised drones, powered and commanded by some great central computer beamed into their neural cortices by infrared and high frequency radio transmitters at every corner of this vast, nightmarish, inescapable maze.

They, and all of society, Malthrop is sure now, are, or are soon to be: slaves of the machine, while he alone, a voice in the wilderness, has constructed a way out, mankind's salvation, an inversion of the universal tyranny, a microcosm in which he at first, and then everyone else, can retake control of their own destiny.

Malthrop returns to his house at last, checking over his shoulder before he unlocks the doors.

Inside, every square foot of his parents' narrow three-storey townhouse, with the exception of the cramped kitchenette, is filled with the enormous Machine begun by his father, built over four decades, blackened cogs and rails and wires and pistons, cutting through propped floors and walls.

He bolts all external doors and windows, closing them over with steel security shutters then prepares himself for the next Cycle Of the Sublime Machine.

He soaks Melanie's clothes in vinegar to preserve them then inserts them, in glass jars, into a new cavity in the Machine's interior. He works with soldering iron, blow torch, nuts and bolts, spanner and screwdriver for two hours, then after a quick electrical test: opens the hall cupboard and steps into the upright Pilot Chamber of the Machine and straps himself in. He activates the Starter with a wire dangling from the ceiling down to his mouth. He bites through it, breaking the safety loop, and the sequence begins. The building begins to shake with the turning of enormous wheels.

Tresses of Melanie's long black hair fall across his face, her winter scarf is drawn across his neck, tightening around his throat, restricting his breathing. A comb made of her teeth springs out and digs into his cheek repeatedly. He cries out. He begins to lose consciousness as the chamber rotates, turning him upside down, blood rushing to his head.

The wheels turn, he drifts. Glitter of light on the horizon. A day at the seaside. Punch and Judy stall, children's laughter. Red and white stripes like a butcher's apron. Bringing two ice creams back to Melanie. Her taking his arm, as they stroll along the promenade. The warmth of her touch, glow of male pride. A ship on the horizon catching his eye.

What is it?—Melanie asks, slightly annoyed at his drifting attention. Silver dancing sparkles of distant waves.

I don't know, it reminds me of something.

The boat . . . . What is it? A trawler? A yacht? A frigate?

Not the boat, the water. The first time I ever saw the sea, taken there by my parents.

Oh Scott, do your father and you miss your mother terribly? Why won't you let me come visit you at home?

The machine steps up a gear, wheels and railways intersect, boiling liquid surges down over Malthrop's face and chest, before he is plunged headlong into seawater. Above him, toy yachts sail

30

back and forth, huge goldfish are unleashed from a neighbouring chamber and they swim towards him, nibbling at his ears. A slithering black eel and crabs are released from another door and his eyes bulge in fear and desperation, running out of air. A timer clicks, turns over and the wheel lifts him upwards into fresh air where he gulps and gasps and yells. Electrodes unfold from the steel walls, bouncing into the water, then charge up, electrocuting him at carefully calculated voltages: agonising but sub-fatal.

His body stiffens and jolts, he passes out. He drifts.

An electric shock, he falls backwards on Melanie's kitchen floor, covered in oil, laughing.

Are you ok?—she marvels, clutching a cup of tea, wearing only a long white T-shirt.

He leans back and flicks a switch, and re-connects a wire. *There, that should do it.* The washing machine drum starts turning, the ballast bricks on top rattling happily.

You've fixed it?

Of course.

Oh Scott, you are good! Is there anything mechanical you can't sort in a jiff? It's not like green fingers, it's sort of like . . .

Grey fingers?

The doorbell goes and Malthrop tenses, always wary of strangers. *Oh who can that be?*

Oh that will just be my brother probably, you can meet him at last . . .

Malthrop makes himself busy as she goes to the door, then hesitates, smearing some more oil on his face, slowing down, reluctant to remove the mechanical distractions and props in front of him, spanners and encasures, plates and switches, bracing himself for the encounter.

The black and white chequered linoleum floor beneath him where he kneels suddenly rises up like a picnic blanket, turns red and yellow then unfolds on a distant green moor, thunder clouds appearing on a far horizon.

Do you think it's going to rain, Scott?

Melanie smiles sweetly, knelt over the picnic basket, unfolding sandwiches, pouring them both coffee from a silver flask shining dreamily in the milky afternoon light.

Inside the Machine, dreaming Malthrop inhales deeply from

31

the canister of air infused with heather and grass and moss, criss-crossed with faint tangs of bread and tuna.

The tapes of her voice play and rewind, play and rewind, at different speeds, from concealed speakers above him. *No, Mel, I think we'll be alright for another hour or so,* he mumbles, *unless the wind changes . . .*

Picnics make me think of my mother, Scott. She used to love them.

What happened, Mel, to her, afterwards, I mean?

After my father's accident? Melanie's eyes fill briefly with fear. Malthrop watches the sweetly scintillating shiver of death flicker over her, like an infusion of ink into a solution, snake venom into lemonade. *Looking back on it now, oh I suppose she died of a broken heart, Scott, over the following few years. She tried, but in the end I don't think she could live without him. Couldn't forgive God or couldn't dare to believe in God in case she couldn't forgive Him, or suffocated, trapped between those two ideas. Sadness is like a sickness that can eat away at someone's soul, until nothing can lift them out of it.*

Not even bird's song on a summer's day?—Malthrop asks, as chaffinches dart over his head, right on cue.

Not even that, no. Do you think you and I could ever love each other that much, Scott?—Melanie asks, and he takes both her hands and her eyes fill with tears. He shuffles closer to her across the grass and embraces her, feels the sudden sadness reverberating within her, tries to absorb it and contain it like a net, focussing it like a mirror.

Seralta and Merkiel pick themselves up off the floor inside the sarcophagus and fly over to either side of Malthrop's cockpit. He remains trapped within, apparently static, entombed and fossilized in an alternative timeflow. *Who was that girl in that scene? The whole room was haunting, strangely familiar.*

I don't know . . . Merkiel frowns, *but I felt it too, as if someone were walking over my grave.*

How do we get through to him? Can we release him?

I don't know, that might be dangerous. He seems to be caught in the middle of some kind of sequence.

Is he trying to reach us?

I don't think he's even aware of us. He seems to be auditing himself, re-ordering, perfecting his own memories . . .

Can we escape, withdraw?

Right now? Not even if we wanted to, probably, I doubt it . . .

Melanie's brother Mitch enters the room and hands her a mug of coffee. A window is open and summer evening sounds spill back into the room, while the shadow patterns of gently moving branches and leaves shift and flicker on the opposite wall. *Sis, I've been meaning to say . . . no insult intended, but I'm not too sure about that new boyfriend of yours. He's creepy . . .*

Melanie shivers, seems to see a flash like lightning at the corner of her eye. The floor wavers, turns into an ocean, turns back. She tenses.

What?—Mitch asks.

A dog barks three times outside then whines.

Didn't you feel that? It's got suddenly colder in here, and I've got such a weird feeling . . .

A fly enters the room through the window then slams into the wall and drops to the floor, legs upturned like a broken toy.

Déjà vu? A premonition?

MECHAGNOSIS #03

~ *Mapping A Face* ~

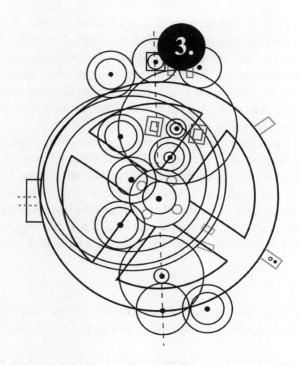

"Every angel is terrible. And still, alas, knowing all that I serenade you, you most deadly birds of the soul . . . "
—Rainer Maria Rilke, from the *Duino Elegies*, #2.

Malthrop runs his hand across the bleached white skeleton of his father and his grave suit, drilled and bolted into the midst of a complex array of wheels and turbines, a private industrial tomb inside the Machine of his family's consciousness. Time to set it going again, he closes over the chamber's steel door, then climbs the gantry to his own place in the cockpit, from which each new sequence can be set in motion.

He turns the dials and levers, makes some adjustments, splices in some new material: flowers stolen from city parks, several dead birds, embalmed. A silver tea set. Straps himself in and throws his head back. The Machine slowly hums and growls into life, beginning its endlessly random and unpredictable cycle. The building shakes, the world outside fades: passing buses and cars, mumble of late traffic and voices. His eyelids flutter. He fades.

Inspector Wroclaw invites Mitch into his office and offers him coffee from the dismal dispensing machine in one corner. They sit down.

Mister Cheswick . . . Mitchell, how can we be of assistance today?

The lines on the old detective's face are a fabulous map of geological time, a dried riverbed after a biblical flood, Mitch muses. *My sister, missing person, Melanie Cheswick, have you any news?*

Wroclaw shakes his head sombrely, *-we would have told you if we had.*

And this guy, Malthrop, that I told you about. Scott Malthrop. Have you found him or found out anything about him?

Wroclaw sighs and leafs through the slim folder on his desk. *Malthrop, friend, boyfriend, occupation probably jeweller, resident probably somewhere in Kentish Town or Camden. I've had more to go on . . . I mean, if I had more to go on, perhaps . . . Mister Cheswick.*

But there must be a guild of jewellers for instance, and a register of all

36

the residents of that name in Camden?

Certainly, Wroclaw nods, *all of these records and others exist, and we have checked them all, but this gentleman shows up in none of them. London is a large and complex place and we have the Freedom of Information Act to contend with. But yes, he may still exist, even if we just happen to be unable to locate him on any of our radars, as it were.*

Now Mitch smiles broadly, if a little sourly. *Oh I know he exists, Inspector, not least because I saw him yesterday.*

Wroclaw's eyelids lift a little at this, his blue eyes shaking off their everyday mist of boredom for a second, as he reaches for a pen. *Where and when was this?*

In a market in Camden, then at my house, he came back to my house.

Wroclaw looks surprised. *Did you tell him we'd like to question him?*

I tried to be subtler than that, Inspector. I hoped he would wait at my house long enough for two of my friends to turn up so we could detain him, shall we say, or persuade him to talk to you . . .

I take it this strategy proved flawed?

Mitch nodded. *He escaped across my neighbour's roof in the fog, carrying two of Melanie's dresses with him. I presume he escaped into Kensal Green Station.*

We'll get in touch with London Underground and get a look at the tapes.

Then you agree his behaviour sounds incriminating?

Possibly . . . it's an easy conclusion to jump to, obviously. Bereaved people behave strangely . . .

Mitch raises an incredulous eyebrow.

But trophies, you're thinking, serial killers, all that sort of stuff. It does seem extraordinarily brazen, careless even, of him, if this is a killer. And you were very unwise to behave the way you did.

Sorry?

This man may be dangerous. You should simply have contacted us immediately.

And watched him run away? You can't be serious. What's wrong with you people?

I understand, Mister Cheswick. Please don't get upset. But we just don't want another disappearance or murder on our hands.

Really? You don't seem all that bothered about this one to me.

Wroclaw's face widens, its wrinkles opening up, into a kind of blank bewilderment, usually his forerunner to anger or contempt.

I'm sorry, I didn't mean that.

Please take this paging device, Mister Cheswick . . . Mitch. I'll get my secretary to programme it for you on the way out. My advice is that you immediately contact us, through this device, should you ever see Malthrop again.

Mitch nods.

And tell me something else: how did this man's mental state strike you? In fact, let's go back to the beginning and record everything he said to you . . .

Malthrop opens a door in the Machine and steps out into a winter landscape of thick white. The Machine is buried behind him under a drift of snow at the base of a mountainside. Sunset and twilight are coming on. He is stunned by the beauty of the landscape before him. The leafless branches of trees, the frozen streams, the fronds of wild grass combed like hair and set hard with hoar-frost. He moves out across the white fields under a broad blue twilight overhead. The sense of deathly peace pervading Nature is overwhelming. He wants to lie down in this snow and gradually cease breathing. To pass into some profound dream and memory of childhood.

Then he hears his father's voice calling him . . .

Why can't I just have a new plastic sledge like all my school friends have, Dad?—young Malthrop shouts to his father as he pursues him across the snow-clad fields.

Because they are evil, son.

Evil?

Cheap, mass-produced, without care or craftsmanship or love. Here, look at this thing!—his father turns and kneels and Malthrop recoils from the crazed look he sees in his eyes more and more frequently since his mother's death.

Look how the timber is carved, sawn, planed, jointed with dovetails and dowels, bolted carefully to perfectly honed steel runners. Son, a man made this sledge, to last a lifetime, maybe several lifetimes. A man who loved his son, just as much as I love you. Don't you see?

Both their heads turn as nearby children fly by on plastic shells in bright shades of red and yellow.

There is no love in those, no humanity. And they will break, they are designed to break so that other ones will have to be made and bought. It's a form of extortion, dishonesty, chicanery . . . whereas this . . . He puts his hands back on the sledge, *-embodies integrity.*

They don't break, Dad! They're better!

Oh yes they do, son!—his father exults then runs over and jumps on one with a loud crack and runs back again to Malthrop, as the children's crying and parent's protestations start up behind him.

They break!—he shouts, over and over again. *And all that plastic can never decay, it will just lie in shreds in tips and landfills and wound and kill all the birds and animals that ever go near it. While this sledge, if we are ever so foolish to discard it . . . it will just rot harmlessly into compost, while its metal can be melted down and re-used or left to rust into oblivion. You see?*—he smiles maniacally as a snowball glances off his back and an angry parent arrives behind him to put a hand on his shoulder.

Gear change. Humming of the Machine. The scene stops, freezes, fades to sepia, turns red then brown, rusts, dissolves into a scrap yard where Malthrop and his father, slightly older: forage for spare wheels and rails and cogs and pistons.

What are we doing here, Dad?

We're looking for more pieces to add to our Machine, of course.

Is this something to do with us losing Mum, Dad?

No, Scott. Absolutely not. And we didn't lose her. That would have been careless. She died. Call a spade a shovel. Being ashamed to talk about death is a sure sign of materialist hypocrisy. The constant and empty accumulation of wealth can only make sense if people live forever, so death must be denied, along with ghosts and mystery and beauty. Everything ethereal and non-physical must be denied, that's what the empty materialists preach to their children, son, the capitalists. We're not like them though, are we? We admit death, we face it, and we live with it because we know your mother had a soul and she is an angel now, and we sense her presence in our house at night, making the lights dim and flicker.

My friend Vince says that's just old electrics, and we need to re-wire the house.

More capitalist claptrap. He says that because his father's an electrician who goes around telling daft old ladies stuff like that every day, then ripping them off for thousands of pounds of their hard-earned savings. He just wants to pointlessly replace everyone's wiring that's been working perfectly anyway. Our whole society is becoming a religion of robbery, of ripping each other off. Integrity is dying. Perpetual change just means perpetual waste. Which will eventually mean our own extinction.

So Vince's dad is a criminal?

No. He's a model citizen of course . . . in a society of criminals.

What are you then, Dad?

I'm a sane guard, sentenced to death by the inmates in an asylum riot, of course. Here, look at this, see this, son? Know what this is?

An old boiler?

Nearly. It's part of a steam train, discarded after the bloody Beeching report. Listen to this. He blows its whistle and rattles its rusting bell. *A distress signal from a dying world. The sound of craftsmanship and integrity. Pass me my spanners. Let's dismantle this thing and get the best bits of it into the car. I reckon we can make good use of this back at the house.*

Mitch sits and weeps, side by side with his girlfriend Carrie, who has her arms around him on the sofa, trying to console and understand him and his growing obsession.

This guy Malthrop, I've got to find him again . . . He killed my sister, I know he did, I can feel it.

But you don't know that, Mitch, you can't know that . . . you have no evidence.

Yes I do . . . all that I need . . . it's obvious. And the police are hopeless. That inspector with the weird name, he is completely useless.

Mitch . . . Carrie strokes his arm. *You have to live, you have to let it go . . .*

It? You mean "her"? How can I let my own sister go?

I didn't mean it like that, Mitch, I'm sorry.

My sister . . . I grew up with her for God's sake. She is all I have, Carrie. You have brothers, can you imagine losing them? It's the memories that kill you . . . as if they're getting stronger, nearer every day, not further away.

It's OK . . . it's OK. Carrie says, holding him, rocking him in her arms, *I understand . . .*

Her voice in his ear becomes the voice of Melanie calling out to him as a child: they are both children running through winter trees white with wind-blown frost. She laughs in mock terror as he pursues her. As Carrie holds him tighter, he longs now to catch up with Melanie, running through those trees, to capture her again as he never quite did, to complete this fragment of memory, splicing, to close the tape loop.

Wroclaw's wife Tilda sits in front of the television, turned up too loud to permit any kind of conversation, her entire body and sensory perception trained unremittingly in the direction of the pool of strident light and sound in the corner of the room. *A sewer running through your living room . . .* -one of Wroclaw's religious grandparents had once referred to television, back in Poland. He smiles to himself at the memory of this and gently pulls the living room door over and retreats to his study.

He sits down at his desk and contemplates his several unfinished books: large volumes ranging from scientific fact through to romantic historical novel, via celebrity biography and crime fiction in between. But all of them suddenly seem so dull as to present a complete impasse to his imagination and lexical stamina.

For a moment he nearly switches his computer on to trawl the web for God-knows-what-all, then stops himself, seeing little virtue in this screen over the one enslaving Tilda. He goes to the hall, puts his coat on, takes a last look at Tilda, the eerie light on her enraptured face and intoxicated eyes, then quietly unlocks the front door and steps out into the night.

Without any initial idea of direction, he finds himself walking instinctively south, hands in pockets, collar turned up against the cold. He stops to light a cigarette, stares vacantly into a shop window and asks himself where he is going. From Hampstead he takes the tube to Kentish Town and begins to walk every street, working his way back from the main road. He reaches into his pocket and almost to his surprise finds a map of the streets around Kentish Town and Camden.

Wroclaw walks every street, restlessly hour after hour, marking them off on the tattered map, looking up at every window as if searching the eyes on a stranger's face. His solitary footsteps echo down deserted streets, criss-crossed by wind-blown leaves. Where is the house of Scott Malthrop?—he asks himself again and again. One of these? But which? Would I know when I saw it? Neglected, almost certainly. Curtains drawn, windows bricked up even, he feels pictures emerging in his head, unbidden.

The few observers who pull aside late pastel curtains, disturbed by his footsteps, gaze down for a moment into the dim pools of streetlight through which Wroclaw walks, hat pulled down, features silhouetted, criss-crossed by shadows of branches, briefly illuminated by the headlights of passing cars.

As Wroclaw walks and marks lines on his folded map, somewhere Malthrop works through the night, drawing lines across newspaper cuttings, photographs. Pinning and pasting them to walls, then cutting over, adding, taking away, endlessly segmenting the ongoing collage of the present, the cacophony of daily news, into some glittering jewel, polishing, honing it, re-ordering the zeitgeist of the ephemeral into some puzzle with the resplendent order of a theorem. Over Malthrop's maps and newspaper cuttings, Wroclaw walks like a tiny fly, before Malthrop swats him.

Wroclaw takes a cab home at 3am and looks into the bedroom to see Tilda is asleep. Unwilling to risk disturbing her, he goes to the lounge, pours himself a drink, flicks through endless channels with the sound turned down, lies down on the sofa and puts a cushion under his head.

Winter sunrise. Walking Carrie's dog near the Regent's Canal, Mitch thinks for a minute he catches sight of a figure that looks like Malthrop. This time he doesn't dare call out his name, but moves to follow him as quickly as possible. On Jamestown Road he seems to turn into a side alley, but when Mitch reaches there he turns around to see the same figure a block behind him somehow, moving in the opposite direction.

He hurries on again, following the figure across a footbridge over the canal, but loses him in the shadows, then again: impossibly, finds the figure has reappeared a block away, behind him, but walking towards him.

Carrie's dog seems distressed and restless, so Mitch ties him up then moves away into the shadows to await the approaching figure. This time Mitch gets enough of a glimpse, with the sun coming up, to be certain it's Malthrop, but he turns down an alley before reaching him. Leaving the dog, Mitch resumes his pursuit, running now where necessary from corner to corner, keeping up with Malthrop. Several times again, Malthrop seems to deny physics and jump location too quickly for Mitch to follow, but always remains within sight, as if luring him on.

To his surprise, Mitch sees the door is lying partially open, the footsteps in the snow leading to the threshold. Exhilarated by his good fortune, Mitch forgets for a fatal moment his customary caution, and hearing no sound from within: opens the door and enters the house of Scott Malthrop Junior. The cramped kitchenette is empty, but its one other door on the far wall is hanging open, revealing a tantalising glimpse of esoteric machinery, humming with life.

Drawn by his curiosity at this, Mitch takes a further two steps inside and the door behind him shuts with a sudden finality. He spins around and sees no human hand has closed it, but rather: massive steel bolts and plates are sliding down and across it with ferocious mechanical precision. Mitch tries in vain to halt these, but when he turns around again hears footsteps enter the room.

Malthrop is standing on a metal gangway above him, wearing a World-War-One gas mask and medical overalls, and the breastplate from a suit of antique armour.

Welcome, Mitchell . . . -the distorted voice rings out from behind the filter, *-to the Museum Of Mechanical Eternity. You should be proud. I've prepared a place for you, as Melanie's only brother . . . you will be enshrined, immortalised.*

Malthrop, is that you? You freak!—Mitch spits in fury, trying to find a way up. *What did you do to my sister?*

The kitchenette ceiling is only a white bedsheet held taut by wires on some kind of pulley system that now begins to drag it aside.

Several clocks on the kitchen walls begin moving forward at speed, their hands emitting a curious whirring noise.

Mitch tries to run forward but finds his limbs unexpectedly weak and falls to his knees. He coughs and looks down at his hands which seem to be suddenly wrinkling as if ageing. *What's happening?!*—Mitch wails.

Time is happening, the distorted voice of Malthrop says sadly. *Time is your murderer, and mine, and Melanie's, Mitch. I'm just the undertaker, the embalmer . . .*

As Mitch's eyesight begins to fail, his bones cracking under his own weight, he looks up to see the vast three-storey façade of the Machine coming to life. Cogs and wheels turning, dials glowing, infinitely complex esoteric functions getting underway, as Malthrop moves around maintaining it, walking the gantries like a priest in his pulpit, a captain of some unfathomable ship.

For a moment Mitch thinks he sees human bones for pistons, teeth for cogs, long hair as drivebands up above, and all around him as he passes out: tanks of acid bubbling, bandages and fresh poultices, moulds and preservation jars, formaldehyde, dissection equipment.

Wroclaw sleeps on his sofa, his beeping pager unheard, a bottle of cheap scotch three-quarters empty on the table beside him, the television turned down, playing some late night quiz show, unwatched. The lines on Wroclaw's sleeping face are vast and complex, twisting and criss-crossing like tracks in the snow, fortune-lines on a palm offered up, irresolvable, a crossword puzzle bereft of clues.

Across the tracks on Wroclaw's face: Malthrop plays in his sledge, led by his father. Mitch chases his beloved sister through ice-frosted trees, calling after her, throwing snowballs. The landscapes fuse, two slopes on the same hill. Like a deadly creek filled with ice: the creased line of Wroclaw's enormous mouth twitches beneath them, breath seeping from his nostrils like a forgotten breeze, bearer of lost dreams of happiness.

Then the rhythm of his breathing suddenly breaks, his eyes flick open wide like two lakes, black ice frozen over, dark and

44

treacherous to walk across, just about to thaw.

MECHAGNOSIS #04

~ *Remember Babel* ~

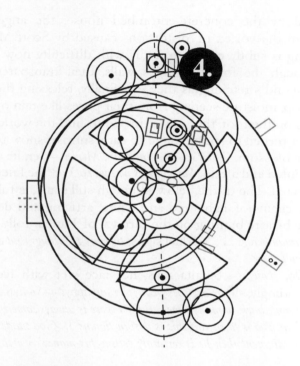

"*If the dangerous archangel took one step now down toward us from behind the stars our heartbeats rising like thunder would kill us. Who are you? Creation's spoiled darlings, among the first to be perfect, a chain of mountains peaks and ridges red in the morning light of all creation, the blossoming godhead's pollen, joints of pure light, corridors, staircases, thrones, pockets of essence, ecstasy shields, tumultuous storms of delightful feelings then suddenly separate mirrors gathering the beauty that streamed away from them back to their own faces again . . .*"
—Rainer Maria Rilke, from the *Duino Elegies*, #2.

Confused by the concrete-entombed house, the angels back away from the vortex of distortions caused by Scott Malthrop. Something is subtly changing. Only with difficulty now do they pass through the four-foot thick walls, their transparent skins puckering and stretching as they exit finally, releasing them with a quiet pop, moisture seeping from their pores like rain or tears.

Up on the roof they are surprised to find the world moved on, winter turned to spring, night to early sunrise, snow to cherry and apple blossom. *What's happening to us, Merk?*—Seralta asks, her voice haunted and afraid. *Something's wrong, isn't it?* She kneels at his feet, dejected. The traffic below, although still static, is fuller now, the daisy chains of lights red and white, arriving and departing, like some bizarre bunting on the carnival of human folly.

Human beings . . . Merkiel sighs, *they are the things that are always wrong, aren't they?*

Why, though?—Seralta asks, her face wet with tears, eyes raised pleadingly, *-Why are they always so unhappy?—So dysfunctional?*

We come back so many times, and yet there is always something new to appal us. But who is to say all this is dysfunctional? If God made mankind for his entertainment then he is certainly getting his money's worth, wouldn't you say?

But this case is affecting us, Merk, isn't it?—Seralta asks, standing up again on the roof beside him, resting her head on his shoulder, looking back down at the faint glow within the concrete tomb where Malthrop's energy still pulses and flickers. *It affects us somehow. It is affecting us somehow. I can feel it.*

Perhaps . . . Merkiel concedes sadly, then takes Seralta's hand. *So let's get away for a while. That sun is coming up, albeit so slowly it will take a hundred years for us. Just think . . .* -Merkiel gestures with a broad sweep of his hand towards the street below. *To them, our lives last but a second, while they spend all their lives thinking the reverse.*

If they think of us at all.

Seralta and Merkiel take to the air and fly south, skirting

Regent's Park and Hyde Park, admiring the treetops, making their way towards the blossom-strewn streets of Kensington and Chelsea. The whole horizon is almost green with morning haze, bands of orange and yellow above it as the ruby red orb of the sun stares the world down like an unblinking eye. The chill breeze of dawn runs through Seralta's golden hair like caressing the strings of a harp.

Oh someone always still thinks of us somewhere, every day.

And when they stop? Seralta asks, beating her wings like the sails of a silver galleon, a little of the old light-heartedness returning to her voice.

Then we will still be here . . . waiting, Merkiel smiles with serenity, the awakening sun lighting up his eyes.

Malthrop sits on his rooftop, cradling a wounded dove in his arms, a tear running down his cheek. Above him the morning sky is brightening into a vast canvas of cirrostratus and vapour trails, whipped and frothed by high altitude winds, like God making a cappuccino laced with blue Curaçao of spring sky. A display just for him. As if. Below all the other lids and roof, Malthrop feels: everyone else moves blindly, hurries through their weekday streets drunk on the vanity of their own importance. An entire city is a machine, yes. But to what purpose? Steam and sweat and dust rise to heaven from their labours, or fall to earth, but what of dreams? The only meaningful product of the machine of humanity must surely be this most invisible of distillations and somehow the least celebrated: dreams, aspirations.

The dove twitches in his hand, a daylight moon catches his eye, as if to answer his thoughts. He takes the bird below and works at his lathe and vice for an hour to repair its wing with balsa and wire, an intricate and ingenious structure, adhered with love. When he is finished he opens a window and sets it free, sighing. It wings its way awkwardly but rapidly adjusting, crossing the streets and re-entering the sky. He wonders if anyone will ever notice, or be dazzled by, this half-machine bird.

On the wall behind Malthrop, the tom cat that attacked the dove still writhes, strangulating slowly on a wire noose, its blood staining the wall.

Tilda wakes and reaches an arm out to explore the empty recess in the mattress beside her. She gets up and wanders through the house in her dressing-gown and curlers. She finds Wroclaw on the couch, as is so often the case, but pauses for a change, and kneels down, leaning closer to examine his face in the muted light from the drawn curtains. For a moment he reminds her of a child, perhaps the child they never had, the innocence of sleep. All the things she sometimes longs to tell him, how proud she is of his work and how doggedly he pursues the scent of evil in the world. They never talk about his work. They scarcely talk about anything. She has learned more about him over the years from his colleagues, occasional chance meetings, than she has got out of him. How fanatical he is about his work, honest and hardworking.

Light as a feather, she dares to move a hand across his forehead and brush a lock of his grey hair aside. Why does he never talk to her? How do people drift this far apart? When was the critical moment? Was there one key thing perhaps, a decision or word said or unsaid, years ago, that set them both off towards these parallel paths of mutual estrangement. *Estrangement?* Was such a thing possible under the same roof? Possible, it was commonplace. Like Arab and Jew, Muslim and Catholic. Mutual misunderstanding. Human beings are prone to boredom. And when we stop looking at the familiar, we supplant it with shorthand, stage scenery, caricatures. We stop really looking, then the trouble starts.

Tilda stands up and goes to the window and puts her hands on the curtains and wonders whether to draw them aside, to throw light in bright gaudy blades all over her husband, to bathe him in golden warmth, to wake him up.

On a branch outside, a robin cocks its head sideways and looks back at her, chirping some incomprehensible message or warning. Communication. Squandered.

Malthrop sets The Machine going again, his head thrown back by sudden force, the restraint straps digging into him. A hatch opens in the ceiling and he is drowned in pink cherry blossom then popcorn, warm upholstery, coca cola pours over his head, bubbles swarming up his nose. He coughs, he drifts. He is in the cinema with Melanie, one of their first dates. The feature is still to start, he is eating ice cream. Melanie nudges him to look over at a neighbouring row: *Look at that little girl, she's a wee fatty . . . Isn't she lovely?*

The thirty-foot high curtains gradually pull aside, the lights dim. But instead of a film, the screen fills with the enormous image of Malthrop's mother, leaning in close, looking at him, taking out a handkerchief to dab at the corners of his mouth, wiping away chocolate.

He is five years old again, uncomfortable in his school uniform, embarrassed by his mother fussing over him, brushing away every speck of dust off his clothes, obsessed with tidiness.

Breaking free at last, he waves goodbye to her and runs to meet his classmates in the playground. Short trousers and socks and satchels, the ringing of the bell, queuing up for classes.

Magpie!—all his classmates call him, teasing, ridiculing, as the teacher empties out his satchel to reveal all the things he has gathered on his way to and from school: pinecones, empty crisp packets, cigarette boxes, a page of newspaper.

Why do you keep filling your bag with rubbish, Scott Malthrop? Are you going to be a street-sweeper when you grow up?

He looks at the floor in embarrassment, humiliated, dejected.

Can't you tell us, Scott, why you keep doing this, does it mean something to you?

Miss . . . he tries to whisper.

Speak up, Scott, explain to the whole class, we're all ears.

Miss . . . I listen to their stories. And as he speaks, his confidence unexpectedly grows, one word following the other, lifting his head up to gaze at the whole class and astound them with his weird exultation. *Objects retain the imprint of the people that make them and use them. Through the objects, I recover the people inside my head, I surround myself with their essence . . .*

Scott! Stop it! Stop this at once! The teacher shouts, mysteriously enraged, slapping his wrist and frog-marching him out the room, oddly ashamed of his eloquence.

Outside in the dismal grey corridor, awaiting punishment, the young part-time teacher walking towards him now transforms into Melanie.

Inside The Machine, leather belts lash across Malthrop in ritual punishment, his face is rammed into a blackboard stained with chalk. The dim chamber he moves through is lit by flickering fluorescent lights, dust-caked, stolen from school corridors. His nose is flooded with the aroma of dismal disinfectants, the smell of weekday tedium, the endless purgatory of school tyranny, enforced education.

The straps pull his head back, stretch his legs. Malthrop grows taller. He is meeting Melanie at her school, after her classes end. *And how were the children today?*

She takes his arm and walks him across the car park, looking over her shoulder. *Oh they were fine, poor little mites, it's Mrs Traverdale I worry about, the old bag.*

Who?

Shhh! Melanie grabs his arm even tighter and pulls him aside, pointing to a grey-haired woman eyeing them suspiciously before getting into her expensive car.

Headmistress. Adolf Hitler in knickers. Even got the moustache.

Mrs Traverdale drives past them and waves from her plush interior, while Melanie curtsies exaggeratedly with a painted smile.

She corners her in the corridor the next day: *Oh, Miss Cheswick, who was that young man I saw you with?*

Young man?

Your husband? Fiancé?

Oh, Scott you mean (feeling lost, embarrassed, Melanie adds:) *He's a jeweller.*

The Commandant's eyes widen, giving Melanie some satisfaction.

He made this . . . -she indicates the watch on her arm, with its curiously exposed mechanisms of interlocking cogs and wheels.

Mrs Traverdale breathes in through her nostrils, lifts her face slightly and nods her head, eyes narrowed, as if suspicious of the curious mechanism crouched like a spider on the beautiful freckled arm.

Somehow the angels find themselves drawn back, unwittingly, unconsciously. As if every thing in existence must have a home to return to at the end of a fine morning stroll and theirs is here. They sit down together again on the roof of Malthrop's house, their wings folded, the pattern of veins and arteries beneath Merkiel's transparent skin somehow almost fusing with the red and white light-chains of cars in the streets below.

Thinking Seralta strangely silent, he turns and to his alarm sees she is sinking helplessly down through the concrete roof, like being eaten by a sofa. She is trying to cry out, gesturing, hands imploring, eyes wide, arms spread, but somehow no sound escapes as Merkiel tries to reach out and hold her back.

Everything is slipping suddenly, there seems nothing firm to hold onto. Merkiel is dragged after her and both angels slowly tumble and slurp down through the concrete chute, like being swallowed by a whale. Down below they emerge into a chamber of flickering light like a wartime cinema over which Malthrop presides like a sacrificial usher, consumed by the flames of his own memories, his goggles misted.

Beneath Malthrop on the floor: the figures of younger versions of himself and Melanie writhe and interlock, naked beneath white sheets that flow and billow like an ocean. As the figures caress and cry out in the throws of passion, the angels are drawn like turbulence, entering the eye of the storm. Become wraithlike, like smoke or mist they encircle and interweave with the bodies and sheets, transmute into notes of golden music, ethereal trumpets and violins, fluttering of angel wings that lick at the walls and ceiling, washing wave-like between plaster cornice and rose.

Melanie and Mitch playing on the beach as children. Golden light and heat. Time pouring by as slowly and luxuriantly as a handful of sand. Red plastic spade and pail, colourful patterned swimsuits. Melanie's hair blonde then, her laughter caressing the air, answered by the pulling cries and wings of the seagulls up above, to whom they glance up, unleashing trails of light-bullets from the swaying sun.

Their parents are there. So close. Mitch looks up and sees them together in the sand side by side on a striped blanket, a fabric windbreaker on stakes behind them flapping in the light breeze from the shore.

He wants to build a sandcastle, to dig a moat around it, to flood with the incoming tide, to show it to his father. But Melanie is crying out now about something, demanding his attention. He turns around and goes to her. She seems bemused, slightly frightened. At the centre of Mitch's sandcastle-to-be, something is emerging, slowly rising up from beneath the sand. In increasing fear and horror, the children huddle together, hold each other and shiver, look around in vain to their parents who are beginning to fade as if behind some opaque screen like an old over-exposed photograph.

The goggled head and shoulders of Scott Malthrop emerge from the sand, then gradually huge wheels and levers also break surface and lift him into the air, sand pouring off in great clouds and rivulets. The Machine rises up from the sand, humming deeply, shaking the ground beneath the terrified children's feet.

Seralta and Merkiel now circle the scene at head height, as fast as atoms or asteroids. They are driven into action. Seralta steps down onto the sand from the white speed-stream and takes the children into her arms.

Merkiel, like the renaissance figure of Da Vinci inscribed by squares and circles: attacks the side of The Machine and spreads his arms and legs to take hold of one of the largest wheels and brings it grinding and groaning to a halt.

One of the wheels begins to buckle until a white light like a sandstorm explodes from its centre and the wheels rewind into the beach. The scene is wiped by the sandstorm into a barbecue on the beach, the Machine transformed into a bonfire and scattering of other blackened fragments all around it.

Nearing sunset, Melanie and Mitch are teenagers now, with six or seven of their mutual friends, getting drunk, experimenting, laughing, nervous, a ghetto-blaster playing loud at their feet.

Melanie gyrates her hips in a way Mitch finds vaguely

confusing and unsettling, one of his friends showing an interest in her that he finds troubling. His stomach churning with a queasy mixture of guilt and excitement, as her best friend kisses him and they both trip over, giggling, her hair in his face. She sighs, looks into his eyes, then goes strangely silent. He pulls her head against his chest, ostensibly in fun but also so he can look over her shoulder and keep an eye out for Melanie. Remembering his promise to his father to take care of her, knowing he has transgressed and can discuss none of this later.

Seralta and Merkiel seem to wake up to find themselves sitting side by side on the roof of Malthrop's house, except that now they are sunk half into its concrete surface as if it is deep sand. For a moment the cityscape before them seems to turn into an ocean of cloud, the buildings into jagged rock jutting out of the sand, the cars and pedestrians below like the microscopic progress of tiny crabs and larvae in rock pools and rivulets on a beach at low tide.

Who are these people, Merk? I'm scared. Why can't we escape them? Who is this Malthrop to us?

Remember Babel? Merkiel says sadly, putting his arm around her. *Sometimes it seems, humanity really does stumble upon some method and creates something to rival God. And gets our attention.*

And what then?—she asks.

Then God tears it down, Sera, if he is awakened by it. And damns its architects to ignorance, to speak a thousand tongues.

Or will he go on sleeping?—she whispers to the wind.

The phone suddenly rings and Wroclaw comes back to consciousness with remarkable alacrity, arising with a few rheumatic cracks of limbs from the sofa to dance nimbly through the hall and lift the receiver.

That's it, that's it. Tilda says to herself from where she still watches him from her place by the living room window. The phonecall. The day he phoned me from work to ask me to accompany him to that conference and I said no. And we argued about it for weeks later, or nearly argued about it, argued might have been better. We skirted around the subject. So he went anyhow to his conference without me and years later I found out he'd slept with that little floozy he met there. Yes, maybe that was it. The turning point. When he phoned I should have said yes and gone to his bloody conference and met him half way. Kept that bridge open, not let it tumble away overgrown with moss. Now a ravine filled with a torrent of cold water flows between us, and both of us are too afraid to leap.

What?—Wroclaw has put the phone down now and returned to the living room door, looking in at her. *You were watching me while I slept.*

Yes, Tilda nods, *I was wondering what you were dreaming about.*

The office. I have to go into the station, right now. Something's come up. A disappearance, a potential witness. It might be significant.

Tilda smiles and nods.

I'll phone, Wroclaw says, putting on his coat, and leaves.

The young woman in Wroclaw's office calls herself Carrie Crawford, the fiancé of Mitch Cheswick. Through her tears and hysteria she tells Wroclaw that Mitch has gone missing while taking her dog for a walk, but that she found the dog tied up near a bridge at the Regent's canal.

A dog, you say? Wroclaw asks, getting up and sitting on her side of the desk and offering her a handkerchief. He hates himself for noticing how incredibly beautiful she looks as she cries, her long straw-blonde hair like a frozen waterfall of sorrow, of yellow autumn leaves. *A dog?*

Yes. Carrie nods her head.

How well does the dog know Mr Cheswick? Have you been seeing each other long?

About a year, she stutters, the answer to both his questions.

Good. Wroclaw frowns, *-that could be very useful.*

Why? Carrie asks, turning her glorious blue eyes up towards him like a source of divine hope.

That could be useful because . . . if you're OK about it, we could get some officers and take your dog back to the scene, with you there as well obviously. But the police dog-handlers might be able to get your dog to show us some things we can't see with our inferior noses.

See with noses . . . .? Carrie starts to repeat, but there is a sudden loud bang and both she and Wroclaw jump, almost embracing each other. Wroclaw crosses to the window and sees that a bird has just hit it. Before its stunned body slips off the window sill and drops to the street below, Wroclaw imagines for a second that he sees timber and wire interwoven with one of its wings, as if it has been repaired by a madman.

MECHAGNOSIS #05

~ *Eternal Saturdays* ~

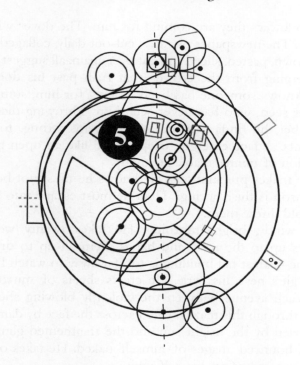

"*O take it, angel! Pluck it, this small-flowered healing herb and go get a vase for it, preserve it! Put it with those joys that still aren't open to us, praise it in a lovely urn with a florid soaring inscription: an acrobat's smile . . .* "
—Rainer Maria Rilke, from the *Duino Elegies*, #5.

Malthrop knows they are coming for him. The doves whisper it in his ear. The newspaper pictures, cut-out daily, collaged, turned upside-down, pasted, sliced and cut over again: all suggest another face emerging from the crowds that rush past his door every day. He knows someone has been looking for him, someone he has never seen, who has never seen him. Throwing dice across an alphabet, he finds a name, but it seems wrong, too many consonants. A face emerges, deeply lined like an open palm, an intersection of unimaginable geometry.

He makes preparations. He knows he must not be found. What season is this? Spring? Then he must escape into autumn, that should throw them.

A windy, bright morning. He takes twenty wet white bedsheets up to the roof and hangs them all up to dry in the wind. The nearest tall building is too far away to watch him here in his eagle's nest, his eyrie. He erects sheets of mirror at the end of each avenue between the violently blowing sheets, and wanders through this maze, beaten across the face by damp cloth, eyes dazzled by the bright sun and the fragmented glimpses of recessive bounced images of himself naked. He takes out a pot of emulsion and paints himself white.

As evening and twilight come on, his skin is still not dry, but tacky. He goes below and rolls himself in autumn leaves then bird feathers.

He straps himself into the Machine and adjusts its dials to maximum acceleration. He nudges the Starter and his head is thrown back instantly. The world lurches into a blur. The crowds outside, the ceaselessly passing, tireless feet, the hum of human electricity. He becomes one with the energy of it, the hidden heartbeat, the beating rhythm under the floor of life. Malthrop is blood now, electric neon pulse, fifty frames a second, excitement of eternal Saturdays, essence of urban life dissolved in pure light.

Inspector Wroclaw has two assistants, one male, one female. Brian Lindsay and Lynn Brien. The odds against this deserve to be run through a super-computer. But how can you send your assistant back to the Superintendent on the grounds that her name is wrong? That's a form of discrimination they haven't even legislated for yet, but no doubt they're working on it.

Keen to pull rank at all times in order to bolster his weak authority in the face of both their expectations of him as a frail and forgetful old man, Wroclaw would like to call the boy Lindsay and the girl Brien. But when he says Lindsay, the girl thinks he means her, and when he says Brien the boy jumps, confidence boosted momentarily by the apparent familiarity. First names would of course, induce a similar confusion, even if he was inclined to use them. Son and Dear, though tempting, would play into their hands by instantly caricaturing himself as a patronising dinosaur. It's impossible. He's hamstrung. He can't relate to them as human beings even if he wanted to, and all because of chance, chance and their bloody names. He's tempted to use the numbers on their lapels, but that would probably only confuse him until he forgot his own mobile or his pin number. No. He just has to look at them one at a time. And shout. Directionally.

Carrie's dog Haselitz, a black schnauzer, is set loose from where he has waited with the police by the canal. Overjoyed to see Carrie, his attention is only gradually brought back to bear on following Mitch's scent.

His ears prick up, his snout twitches, then he begins to lead the handlers away into the side streets near the canalside. Carrie lifts her eyes and Wroclaw meets her gaze, absorbing the fear and anguish in it.

You better stay here, Miss Crawford, with the WPC, in case we need your help with your dog. We'll keep you informed of anything we find.

Haselitz and the specialist police team zig-zag through streets for an hour, sometimes losing the scent, sometimes giving up and starting to return to the bridge, when a new fragment of scent is apparently found and another pursuit begins.

Eventually, where Wroclaw and Carrie stand together at the bridge, a radio message is received and Haselitz is brought back to be reunited with Carrie.

No use then? Carrie sighs bleakly over her paper cup of coffee.

On the contrary, Wroclaw looks down at his feet, stubbing out a cigarette. *He's led the team to a quite likely address, apparently. We're going to surround it and make a raid, but the place for you is going to be back at the police station. You'll be quite comfortable, and we'll let you know how things go. This could conceivably be dangerous, but either way it shouldn't take more than an hour or two to check out.*

Thank you, Carrie says, placing her hands on his arm.

No, Wroclaw stops her, *don't thank me until we see how this works out.* His eyes are dark and clouded with grim possibilities, hers are red and wet with tears.

Wroclaw stands at last, flanked by police officers, before the house of Scott Malthrop Junior, and knows he has found his quarry.

Strange place, isn't it, Sir?—his sergeants confer.

Peculiarly narrow house, yes. Wroclaw looks up, eyes squinting in the early spring sunlight. *Windows seem boarded up, almost like a disused building. Yes, this might fit. The dog followed the scent right to the door?*

Yes, and our dogs have confirmed it, using one of Mister Cheswick's T-shirts.

OK then, I'll stand over there. Knock once, usual warning, then break the door down.

The force of their own impact with the steel door nearly injures the police team, expecting the door to flex. No give. Loud hailers are deployed, the wall scaled with ladders instead, windows tested.

Twenty-four hours later, the street cleared and pneumatic drills brought to bear, the police enter through a ragged hole cut in the wall at first floor level. They emerge from the dust a minute later and look down at Wroclaw. *Sir, I think you'd better come in and see this.*

Have you cleared the building? You're certain there's no one inside?

Sir, it's hard to explain until you see it. This isn't going to be an easy house to search. We can make it secure, there's no way out that we haven't got covered . . . the sergeant pauses as he gets a message on his radio. *They've opened a hatch on the roof from the inside apparently. We can go in from the top now and work our way down.*

Up on the roof, Wroclaw is dazzled by all the white sheets, some of them now fallen onto the concrete. *What's that smell?*

I think it's ammonia, Sir. We think the sheets were all soaked in ammonia.

Why ammonia?

The sergeant shrugs his shoulder.

I'll tell you why . . . Wroclaw says, kneeling to unfurl a sheet. *It's sensitive to ultraviolet light, like in the Ozalid printing process. These are like photographs, look at this shadow burnt across the fabric.* Wroclaw looks around and sees the sections of mirror still resting against the parapets. *I think this guy was taking snapshots of himself, leaving them for us to find. Except they're multiple exposures, look: that would have been his face there, except he moved or the wind blew the sheet or both.*

Could we get an image of him from these?

Possibly, Wroclaw muses, *but you'd need one hell of an algorithm to de-encrypt the effect of wind turbulence, in fact it might be quicker to calculate Pi. This guy is like some kind of performance artist.*

Descending into the house of Scott Malthrop, Wroclaw finally understands the difficulty in carrying out a conclusive search. Everywhere, over every wall the eyes alight upon: machinery of obscure purpose writhes and intersects, a mechanical engineer's wet dream, a sculptural paean to industrialism.

Wow . . . *what the flaming fuck?*

Astonishing, isn't it, Sir?

Wait, Wroclaw stops, putting his arm on Lindsay's shoulder. *I think I see the problem here, and the solution. Send the boys back to get infra-red equipment, borrow it off the helicopter crew if necessary. This place is cold, whatever this machinery is, it's not doing anything right now, so if there's any human being alive in here, friend or foe, victim or perpetrator, we should be able to find them fast by their body-heat, before we get the spanners and blow-torches out and start dismantling things. Get on the radio, go on, get to it.*

Wroclaw reaches out and pulls open a creaking hatch. *Wait!*

Lindsay returns. *What would you say that piston is made of?*

Bone, Sir.

They look at each other. *Possibly human.*

Get the autopsy team down here as well, full forensics, and close the street. We're going to need a local curfew to keep the press out of here. This could be major.

Next day, Wroclaw tells Carrie Crawford an hour in advance of the statement he intends to release to the press: that the remains of at least two adults have been found among the machinery inside Malthrop's house, but it will take several days to confirm their identity through dental records and DNA analysis and comparison with relatives.

But you think one of those is Mitch, don't you? Why don't you just say it?

It's early days yet . . . he starts to try and say.

Mitch and Melanie, it's obvious isn't it?

We need to be sure, Carrie. I'm sorry, we must deal only in verifiable facts.

Can't I see his body and identify him?

No. I'm sorry, Carrie, that won't be possible or appropriate.

Why not? Stop soft-soaping me, Inspector. I'm going to read it all in the frigging papers soon enough anyway, amn't I?

You just have to wait. I'm sorry, that's all I can say right now, the forensic analysis of the scene is ongoing, a few days for answers, that's all.

What about Scott Malthrop? Has he escaped?

We've carried out an infra-red scan of the entire building. There is nobody alive in there. So Malthrop either escaped before we got there or . . .

Or what?

Wroclaw shrugs. *Or killed himself, I suppose.*

Why are you so uncertain about everything? Can't you see who's in there, what's it like?

Carrie, it's full of machinery, that's all I can tell you. Weird machinery, wheels and pistons, some of them apparently very old. It's like nothing any of us have ever seen before. A real mess. But I can assure you again there is nobody alive in there.

Assure me? Carrie starts to shake and sob. *Just my Mitch dead and cut up or something, is that what you're skating around?* Carrie sits forward and puts her head in her hands until Wroclaw and WPC Lynn Brien move closer and put their hands on her shoulders. Wroclaw signals with his eyes and sends her out of the room to get more tea.

In the afternoon, Wroclaw is told of a particularly insistent tramp having turned up at reception. *Some old nutter, can't you get rid of him, threaten him with a few byelaws?*

He mentioned the name Malthrop, Sir. Scott Malthrop. That name hasn't yet been given out to anyone, not to any of the press.

No . . . neither it has . . . that is interesting. Wroclaw sighs. *Is he . . . you know, sanitary? Sane? Safe, relatively, to talk to?*

Usual stuff sir, rambles a bit, incoherent, but pretty much sober right now we think. Could be mad as a hatter of course, but so could half the people that pass through this station.

And most of the staff . . . Wroclaw murmurs, *OK, let him in, bring him into Mission Control for a few minutes and we'll hear him out, listen to his ramblings. Make sure he wipes his feet, oh and Lynn?*

It's Lindsay, Sir, I'm the male one. Yes?

Put a plastic sheet over that chair, would you, first? I don't want to be savouring his aroma for the next three weeks . . . And send Brien in.

I'm Brian, Sir.

Shut up. You know what I mean. The girl . . . she's not you in drag, is she?

Name?—Wroclaw begins.

Most folk call me Wilbir.

Most folk call me the old cunt who runs this place, but I do also have a name my mother and father gave me.

Ah never knew my mother and father.

Wroclaw raises an impatient eyebrow.

William James Birnam, as in "Fear not 'till Birnam Wood do come to Dunsinane . . . "

Wroclaw is surprised and impressed. *You have an above average knowledge of the works of William Shakespeare, for a homeless drifter, no offence. Macbeth I believe, the bard's timeless meditation on the inevitability of fate and the tricks destiny plays on each of us.*

No offence? That's a nice touch, guv, oh ah like the cut of your jib alright . . . no offence, indeed. If only all your men had your manners.

They treat you roughly?

Not at all, guv, not today I mean, not in here, it's just . . .

Generally, society . . . everyone . . . you're invisible or a nuisance to most people, that's what you're going to tell me?

Invisible would be alright, guv, I don't have to beg much, I can get by, I can look after me self. But coppers harass me. We're the scapegoats to them, us and the young black guys, the soft option when they want to sound off and dish out some shit . . . no offence, guv.

OK, enough sociological pleasantries, Mister Birnam. What do you know about our crime scene in Clevedane Lane, other than what you read in the papers?

Oh, I don't read them, guv. I sleep on them and wrap my feet in them. I got better stuff than that. I met this geezer Malthrop you're looking for. Years ago, I seen him lotsa times, before he became a recluse. Oh yeah, I knew Malthrop alright.

Where did you get this name Malthrop from? We've given out no such information.

That house is pretty unique though, innit? The Spite House, they used to call it, last century. The old story went that it was built so narrow by some old Victorian geezer, eighteen hundreds, trying to piss off a property developer who wouldn't give him the price he wanted. Sounds familiar? Nothing new under the sun, ain't that the truth. That house is scarce ten feet across, but more than thirty deep.

So you stood outside and paced it out this morning, big deal? You're telling me this man Malthrop owned this house. Nothing I don't already know. Tell me when you knew him, what year was this?

Oh, Thatcher government, early eighties . . .

Wroclaw shakes his head. *Not our man.*

No? Ain't you heard of reproduction?

66

Sorry?—Wroclaw frowns.

He had a son, you know. Maybe you lookin' for the son, but ah knew his daddy-oh.

With the same name?

Yeah, why the hell not? Junior, he called the boy, Scott Junior. As Birnam smiles, Wroclaw's eyes widen a little. *Ah . . . ah got ya hooked now aint I? Ah got me a story you wanna hear, don't I?*

Maybe . . . Wroclaw nods reluctantly.

Any chance of a bed for the night, Inspector?

How does a cell sound?

Cold and hard.

Yeah, just like me. Tell me what you know. If the story's good then we'll get your dinner brought in. Fish and chips.

I was thinking Chinese.

Were you? A wino on the make. Thatcher would be proud. God give me strength. No, we'll buy British on my watch if you don't mind. Now sing if you please, you aromatic old canary, my upholstery tires of you already.

The tape starts . . .

MECHAGNOSIS #06

~ *The Testament of Wilbir* ~

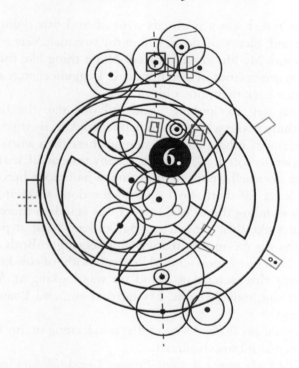

"Wasn't this like a miracle? Gaze at it, angel, it's us, you mighty being, you tell them that we could accomplish such things, my breath isn't enough for such celebration . . . "
—Rainer Maria Rilke, from the *Duino Elegies*, #7.

Listen guv'nor, I was a posh city gent once. I was doing alright. Designer pad, plenty of dosh, still in my twenties. Was gonna get hitched soon. My life looked sorted. Not a thing like the shabby ragbag you see in front of you now, nah. Begging change on street corners, not back then, not a bit of it.

I was set up, looking good, 'til one day the damndest weirdest thing in the whole world happened. Utterly threw me. So mind out, cos' if it happened to muggins here then who's to say it can't happen to you n' all, anytime . . . any time at all, mate.

The doorbell went one morning, a half hour before I was going to leave for work. So I opened the door and who do you think was standing there? Me, mate, I was standing there, myself, but looking like this: captain ragbag, looking back at posh City boy putting his tie on. My flaming doppelganger. Both our eyes widened and our blood chilled to ice. Both of us knew, see, straightaway this weren't no fraud we was looking at. This was real weird shit, twilight zone. My head swam, and I saw he was stunned too.

Recognise me, Wilbir?—he said at last, leaning on my door like he half owned it himself already.

Wilbir? My name's William Birnam, I said, *I'll have you know*, I probably added pompously, all high and mighty.

That's what you call yourself now, he sneered, *but in the future everyone will call you Wilbir, including yourself.*

Who are you?—I asked frostily, *and how the hell would you purport to know about my future?*

Simple, he says. *I am you, from your future. Look*, he says, and bares his left arm and shows me two freckles then makes me roll up my shirt sleeve to show some identical. Then he told me my childhood nickname had been *poggy* and the names of all the towns my parents ever took me to on holiday and the names of the first girls I ever fancied.

Jesus, my head began reeling, *-Identical twin, is that what this* *is?—But why wouldn't my mum have said something . . .* I stammered, staggering back, as tramp-boy comes in and closes the door behind himself and starts walking around the flat making us both a coffee . . . and of course he knew how many sugars I took.

I sort of collapsed and sat down at the same time, and tramp-me grabs me a seat to make sure I land in it right, then brings me coffee and a glass of water and sits opposite me and beams into my face. I mean, he was real sweet suddenly, and I can't explain how weird it is to have yourself look after yourself like that. Actually, it's pretty good, cos' you realise whatever you think or want, he's going to know and sort it for you.

Who are you and what do you want?—I finally managed to say, my City tie left half-knotted at an angle around my neck like a hangman's noose.

I told you, he says. *I'm you and I've come back from the future to visit you.*

Presuming for a millisecond, I sighed, *that any such scenario is even remotely plausible or scientifically possible . . . why?*

Well, he says, leaning back with an expansive gesture and showing off all the finery of his tattered clothes. *Sort of self-evident, innit? This is what you will become soon enough. I'm the fate you've got waiting for you, son. Your goose is cooked.*

OK then . . . I sipped my coffee and reached to light up a cigarette with shaking hands, even though I'd given up six months previously.

Tut, tut, he shook his head, *-you gave that up six months previously. Of course, I smoke strictly douts and dog ends myself these days, from pavements and waste-paper baskets, much healthier. Pharyngitis I can cope with, but cancer, no thanks.*

Wait a minute, I said, trying desperately to think rationally, my head in my hands. *If you're me from the future then you've already been me. You know already whether I'm going to smoke this or not.*

He smiled broadly, showing various gaping holes between his teeth. *Clever boy, Wilbir, weren't you always, I'm so proud.*

Here, I said in disgust, handing him the lit cigarette, expecting him to stub it out. He handed it back and said *"a last request, gringo", just enjoy yer fag . . .*

Why didn't you take a draw on it?—I asked.

You wouldn't have touched it after if it had been in my shitty mouth, now would you?

I nodded, seeing the logic, and enjoyed the calming effect of the nicotine hit. *A last request?* I asked, a delayed reaction. *That doesn't sound good. Oh shit, this isn't one of those "there can be only one" scenarios, is it?* I managed a smile, and he laughed to see it.

Now we're getting' along better, aint we?—he said. *No, no worries, mate, I'll be gone soon enough, I'll just leave you to your own business. But once I'm gone, unfortunately you're going to start seeing everything differently. Your own life, everybody else's, and before you know it you're not going to want this fancy life anymore, or more to the point: it's not going to want you.*

What is this? A premonition? A curse? I don't want to look like you, live like you, not now, not ever.

Who does, mate? But you'll come to it all the same, soon enough.

I don't believe you and I don't want to. You look older than me anyway. That means I've got years before I end up like you. And anyway, Christ, I can't believe I'm playing along with this madness, you, I mean I, we, can still get out of that mess, can't you? You could sober up, get taken in by a kind old lady, rob somebody wealthy, I don't know . . .

Ah, Wilbir, spare me your sociology lecture. So many questions you don't really want the answer to . . . but I'll give you them anyhow, especially now that I see you being so disrespectful, now that I'm reminded what an arrogant, selfish little asshole you were. I'm fucked and you're fucked, not because of our circumstances but because of the shit in our heads. The shit I've just put there. Once a man loses faith, blind faith I might say, in the lie of our society, then there is no going back. You only get out of your bed because you think you're going to be a fucking millionaire next year, but now that I've told you you're not then everything will gradually unwind for you. Living is a triumph of hope over expectation. Once that triumph turns to defeat, you're stuffed mate. That must be why time was invented. Time is the curtain between our two selves, past and future, and whoever draws it aside goes instantly mad.

An old wino philosopher . . . God preserve us.

I'm only ten years older than you, I'm sorry to have to tell you. Well, not really sorry to be honest. It's a bit of a fun shocker revelation, that one, innit? Life on the streets sure ages a man. You'd like to think from this face that I'm an old man, but I'm not, I can assure you. It doesn't take long once things start falling apart, the moment you walk out of here basically, before

Lizzy gets irredeemably pissed off with all your metaphysical speculations and depressions. That's when you realise how shallow your relationship is, and how she's only into you for your money, the vapid little . . .

Hey! Don't talk about my girlfriend like that!

Our girlfriend, your girlfriend, well whatever, what's the fuss? You'll be talking about her like that too in a few weeks . . . Tramp-man stood up.

Where are you going? And why have you done this? Why not leave me alone?

Don't you get it?—he laughed and took the tail end of the cigarette from me and finished it. *I need you to give birth to me, or I don't get to exist.*

You fucker!—I started to fume, standing up.

Ahh, the moment when you try to kill me . . . . He muttered, *yes I remember it all so clearly.*

What?—I said, wrong-footed by his ambivalence.

No need to kill me, mate, this is the bit where I save you the trouble. You're going to like this. Follow me.

Follow you? This is my flaming flat, for Christ's sake, where do you think you're going?

To the shower of course. I don't smell too hot, right?

Hold on a minute, this is my flat.

Our flat, sunshine, but not for much longer, granted. Look, like I've told you, I'm leaving in a minute, what more do you want?

I followed him through the house, and yes of course he somehow knew exactly where everything was. *You can't just do this,* I said, *-come barging into my house and tell me my whole life is about to crash. Hey what are you doing?*

Stripping off of course, man, you can't expect me to take a shower clothed. What you looking at? Yeah, that's right, I'm exactly like you, mirror image, here take off your shirt too, see that birth mark?

Hey, what is this?

Relax . . . he said, stepping into the bath. *I'm not going to offer to blow your cock and then have a chilled-out philosophical debate afterwards about whether it was a homosexual act or not.*

Please . . . I grimaced.

No. Begging me won't help, I won't do it I tell you, I'm too busy, I have to go very soon, as I keep telling you. But you'd be surprised at some of the sordid things that you, I, we, have to do in the future just to get some money for food from one day to the next. Now watch this . . .

He switched on the shower and something utterly astounding happened, the likes of which I have never seen before or since. As each droplet of water hit him he was erased by its impact. He looked and laughed at me and waved goodbye as bit by bit, in spray after spray, he erased himself from reality. I still remember the almighty clunk at the end as the shower-head simply dropped from his vanishing hand and crashed onto the steel surface of the bath below.

I staggered backwards and collapsed onto the toilet seat, and just sat there dumfounded in silence for an hour, as the early morning sunlight moved across the floor and failed to rouse me from my introspections. Too late, I saw that the sunlight erased his discarded clothes, turning them to steam as I reached out to hold their last fragments in my trembling fingers.

So the tramp turned out to be right. Of course he did, how could he not be? Oh I fought it, sure I did. I didn't just roll over and die. It took weeks, months. It takes us a whole lifetime to die, I suppose, to fail, if you want to be philosophical about it. Tramp-man had opened up a space inside me, a doubt, a metaphysical blackness that I could share with no one. I tried to stay happy and lightweight, chipper and cheery, living in the moment, going down the pub with friends and laughing our heads off about life and other people. But increasingly my smiles were painted, my eyes always far away. Over the laughing shoulders of my City mates, my eyes would always catch sight of down-and-outs and cripples, all the human debris that we seemed embarrassed to talk about, except to mock them in some inhuman joke or another. Except I couldn't do that anymore. I'd even stop and talk to them and offer them money.

Hey, Birny, what you playing at?—What's with the Mother Theresa act?—they'd rib me. *Birny's acting weird these days, he's hitting on hobos instead of hot babes, the guy's going freaky. You stressing out, Will? Excitement of blue-chip stock messing with your brain or something? What is it with you these days?*

With Lizzy it was even worse. *Talk to me, Will, I don't know what you're thinking anymore. Has something happened? Why don't you talk about it? These black moods where you stare off into space, tell me where you go to inside your head?*

So I finally relented and told her and that was the biggest mistake I ever made—worse even than opening the door that morning to that indigent freak.

You what? You saw a tramp dematerialise in your own shower? You expect me to believe that? Have you had any other hallucinations?

It wasn't a hallucination, Lizzy. I touched the guy with my own hands. He was real, and he was identical to me in every way.

Then it was her turn to go silent. She just sat and stared sideways off into space in some fancy Knightsbridge restaurant, tears coming to her eyes. Everyone must have thought we were having a tiff or I had just told her I was seeing someone else, which I suppose I had, except the someone else was me. *I can't handle this,* she finally said, wiping her eyes, *I can't handle this anymore, Will, you need to see someone, a doctor.*

You asked a question and I answered it truthfully, I said lamely, realising truth wasn't much in demand at that moment, nor perhaps in relationships generally. You see how things build one after the other?

I tried telling other people, reluctantly, or took to making up excuses, pretending I had a mental illness. No such luck, I went to see a shrink and after ten laughable minutes left convinced the guy was madder than me. They all are a bit loopy you know, trick-cyclists, from listening to other people's nonsense all day. At least mine was a frigging blockbuster.

So you get it by now. Do I really have to join up all the dots for you? Eventually I was going home as slowly as possible so as to avoid the empty flat, stopping off at lonely bars where I could tell half-cut strangers as lost and pitiful as myself about my lost and pitiful life. The flat was there, the job was still there, for a while. But they were empty shells now, as if, and now here's the crunch: as if some sleight of hand had happened between me and that tramp, as if before stepping naked into that shower he had somehow swapped himself for me.

Because although I still remembered all the skills I needed for work and who all my friends were, everything was seen through a haze, as if remembered from a distant past. Yeah, just like I had unexpectedly returned to my life from ten tears in the future. Yeah.

Just like that exactly.

So I cocked up at work. I cocked up a lot of times. Put money on the wrong stock, failed to sell it at the right time because I was sleeping in, hung over, or just didn't care. And my reaction to the reprimands were what really swung it: then everyone saw I REALLY didn't care.

Friends stopped calling me. I stopped calling them. It stopped mattering. Again, I didn't care. Clearer every day, I could see the future looming towards me, the one that the tramp had mapped out for me, and like a rabbit in the proverbial headlights, or a prisoner before a firing squad with nowhere to run, I just lifted my chin and looked right ahead into the centre of things and waited for God to come and head butt me.

And he came soon enough. Fired, home re-possessed, spending the last of the money on a three week bash, a couple of prostitutes. Shit, I'd do all that again, if I had any money. That was the right thing to do. Say goodbye to your own life with a big fucking party for one.

What? You wanna know the point of this story? Oh, I ain't done yet, copper. I ain't no tease. I've not just got the mystery to tell you, I've also got the explanation, of sorts, and that's where this guy Malthrop comes in, the one you're looking for. He comes in right on cue.

I ended up living rough of course. For years. Sleeping under bridges. Charing Cross Road. The canalside, Regent's Park. You learn the ropes after a while. It's a life, man. Weird to say, but it's got its own rules. A wino works to stay alive like anyone else, just like you do. Say, how many days d'you get off? We ain't so different. You slave night and day to scrape together enough to live on and eat, and whatever else you and your fancy wife thinks you really need, but it's a treadmill for all of us, you and me. Only kings and sultans and shit get to sit around all day and there's damn few of them left I dare say. Even them pop stars seem to worry away trying for their next feeble comeback these days, to fund their drug habit or whatever. Man, life's a cycle of shit and there's no escape from it for any of us.

What's that? Yeah, copper, that's right. Even the stars without drug habits, they're itching to get a come back too, ain't they? Even though they can't need the cash that much. So what do they need? Don't you get it? What do we all need? If it ain't food and drink then its self-respect and vanity, and don't underestimate them things. Nobody can live for long on one of those without the other. Look at all them fancy Hollywood women and pretty-boys with their plastic surgeons trying to cheat wrinkles and ageing and death. We're all on the same sinking boat, my friend, riddled with holes cos' that's how God made it, no matter how you look at it.

I was saying. The point. Yeah, I'll get there, hobblin' along at my own good pace. I was sleeping rough under Macclesfield Bridge, with a group of other geezers. The half of whom are pegged by now, the other half: well, who knows? Cos' this guy, Malthrop, who you say might have been the daddy of the Malthrop you're looking for, well whatever, he came by and started up talking to us all, bringing us food and stuff at first. And the others were dead grateful and were well fooled but I seen through him from the start, I saw he had some weird little gleam in his eye.

Mistah, I said. *What's the game with you? What you really up to with befriending us no-hopers?*

No game, he says, *no game, I have a church . . .*

Oh yeah? Now I get it-

No, he says, *it's not what you're thinking. I'm not clergy, not even religious, I've just got this place as a shelter. You guys can all get a roof over your heads and warm up from time to time. All you gotta do is visit this church building and I can show you some stuff I've been working on. I'm an inventor*, he says, *an artist.* And he wasn't kidding. This guy was an artist like none you ever saw before. The whole world ain't ready for the shit he was pulling.

We went there, me and Freddie Fleck, Hoarse Mary and Bert Chappins and a few others, and that's when we saw Malthrop's little boy. There was something well weird about that kid by the way, something I couldn't quite put my finger on. Oh I know lads often look just like their dads but this kid really was the utter spit: the same snigger, the same twisted smile that they'd both smile together at the same time, like they were asymmetric twins, distorted images in a hall of mirrors. He made this poor little mite walk around between the pews where we was sat and take contributions from us. *Contributions*, we laughed! *We're down-and-*

outs, man, we got nothing to give.

Oh yes you have, said Malthrop. *You always got something. Give me a scrap of clothing or a piece of fingernail, give us any tiny thing that means something to you, cos' in there is your essence and that's what I'm after and what I'm about to show you.*

I didn't know if he was a magician or a messiah or a scientist or a plain old common-or-garden nut job, but Malthrop banged on for hours or more every time we went there, ranting he was, about how machines were destroying humanity, now what were that phrase of his "erasing our sense of ourselves" yeah that was his favourite line. He said all them cars and TVs and mobile phones was like idolatry, false gods, that people were worshipping cos' they thought science was their religion now. But Malthrop said all them gadgets were making them soft, dependent, losing the use of their legs and their brains, like big white fat slugs that were all gonna scream and dissolve come the day somebody tossed some salt on them.

Hey why you tellin' us? I heckled him. *We don't own any of that stuff anymore, you've got our vote!*

That's exactly why though . . . he said, all cunning. *Because only you see clearly. You're free of possessions, free of materialism and that means you are opened to the miraculous.*

Opened to what?—we choked. Then we knew something freaky was coming. Malthrop unveiled some weird machine he'd built, right there in front of the altar of that church. It was tall as a man, wide as a bed is long, all black grimy cogs and wheels and chains and shit, weird looking like science fucking fiction, then he started it up. What happened? Oh man, man, how can I ever describe that? The air, the space in front and around it all started to bend and get drawn inwards, even the light and sound started getting sucked into it, like a black hole, and this long narrow plume thing of black dust fired out each side of the wheel in the middle, and left holes burnt into the stone walls of the church afterwards.

We thought it was some magic trick. Maybe it was and I'm crazy or dreamt it all or maybe I dreamt my life and I'm not really here at all. But I swear he brought back the scrap of my shirt to me and showed how he had de-aged it. It was twenty years back in time, this cloth, man, I swear, it was brand new. And then he got

Hoarse Mary's ferret and put that in his machine and brought it back out as a little baby thing. Now where'd he have found a baby ferret on the spot if he was joshin' us? I gave him a rotten apple core with a pin through it and he brought it back to me whole, brand new, luscious, except when we cut it open there was that pin still there down inside, exact same kind with a little coloured plastic head. Oh, that spooked me, then I had the heeby jeebies alright. He caught a pigeon from the church roof then let us all watch as he turned it back into an egg. We watched it hatch later, and it weren't one from down the supermarket, that was the same bird alright.

How'd you pull all this off?—we asked him, *and why you tellin' us? How come the rest of them scientists out there ain't figured this shit out yet?*

He showed us around his machine, opened up all its little doors and chambers and began to explain how this was just a prototype and he was busy building a full size one back at his house. Oh shit, but wasn't it then that the penny finally dropped for me. I suddenly got this big sinkin' feeling, and so did all the others. At first. For a while. Then some of us, the dumber ones I have to say, started getting a bit excited about it.

I could go back then couldn't I?—squawked Hoarse Mary, *and see me dead husband again, old Alf, and bake him steak pie and hump til sunrise!*

Bert Chappins began to dance in the aisles and say he could have his antique business back. He'd go back and murder his business partner before he could steal his wife and embezzle his life savings. I didn't like the way any of this was going. I was watching the sly grin on the face of Malthrop and his creepy little boy and I figured we were putting our heads in the lion's mouth, we was turkeys voting for Christmas.

Hey, I said, trying to catch him out, *if you hate all the machines out there so much, why you building one of your own?*

Excellent question, he smiled. *And the answer is because this machine is the antidote to all the others. Their machines diminish people, but mine will reveal to each of them the ultimate truth of their lives.*

You don't believe a word of this, do you? But I saw it with my own eyes. A few weeks later he strapped old Mary into his machine and disappeared her, right in front of us. Then Bertie the very next night. And I never saw them again, nor some of the other tramps I heard he took and I saw him sniffing around like a crow with carrion. I kept checking the paper and the phone directories I found in doorways, but nothing changed, but would I have known if it had? If Bert had really gone back and managed to bump off his partner and kept his business, then wouldn't that old shop sign now say Chappins & Co outside again, not still say Melrose Tams? And Mary, if she had went and found her first husband and stopped him going to the war, then wouldn't that mean her daughter Caroline by old Jake Hughes would never have got born? But Caroline still exists alright, cos' I see her everyday at the flower stall at Stables Market.

So maybe they never went back, or if they did maybe foresight and foreknowledge ain't all they're cracked up to be, and when you see the same dilemma again you just get caught up in the moment and make the same dumb-ass mistakes all over again. Who knows?

So this is the bit in the story where you expect me to say I was smarter than the others and I figured out Malthrop was a fraud and saw right through him, never had anything more to do with him and was never stupid enough to step into his infernal machine. Yeah, and how I have always wondered "what if?"

Afraid not. How I wish all that were true and I was that smart. Every time I saw Malthrop skulking around, handing out food, chatting up drop-outs, if he saw me he'd get this little smarmy smirk on his face, every time. And over time it got to annoying me so much I finally cornered him and confronted him about it.

So you're time has come at last then, William Birnam?—he laughed.

Hey, how'd you know my old name? -nobody calls me that around here anymore, nobody knows my real name!

Oh, I know a lot of things, Birnam . . . he smiled in self-satisfaction. *I know how to send things through time and I know you're going to be the next thing I send.*

Away and take a flying fuck at a rolling donut, I said. *That ain't true at all, cos' I ain't wanting to go, and if you so much as lay a hand on me I'm callin' the coppers.*

He laughed again and I grabbed him by the throat. *Don't you see?-* he coughed, when I let him down. *-You have to go back or you won't exist. It's unimaginable not to. Us having this conversation at all means you're going back. Don't you remember that day twenty years ago when the doorbell went and that other version of yourself stood there in rags?*

Hey! You fucked-up cut-price wizard! How the hell d'you know that kind of shit about me?

Not my most impressive stunt, surely?—he said, dusting himself down, *-after all, you told every drunk you could find that story every night for two years.*

What is this? Who are you? What are you?—I said, dumfounded.

You have to go back to try to warn yourself, to meet that arrogant young man in the suit again and try a second time to persuade him of how to save his own life, of how to sort himself out before he falls into the abyss.

Again?—I whispered, . . . *Has all this happened before?* I sat down and shook with confusion. This guy was like the great toy-maker tinkering with one if his broken creations. He was like God, the way he spoke, or the Devil, and either way I didn't care much for him or what he was doing to me, pulling my strings like a puppeteer.

Give me one thing then, I said, *if you want me to believe in you.*

Anything, he said, and I realised of course that he already knew whatever I was going to say next.

Show me how your machine works, explain the method.

He took me to a wall inside his church, in the semi-darkness and lit a few candles round about. Then he took a piece of chalk and began marking points and lines, endless lines criss-crossing and curving between them. At first I thought he was going to draw a pentagram or something corny like that, but he just kept going and the shapes and lines got more and more complex and bewildering. *It's all about geometry you see, this is the manual method. The machines just enact the geometry for me, automatically, adding time, the fourth dimension.*

What the hell is it?—I asked, scratching my head.

It's the shape of space-time itself of course, he said calmly, as his chalk rattled methodically across the stone. *You just have to recreate it accurately then reality falls into it. Fortunately, if you get it even near to right then the lines start bending themselves into place. It's completely safe, and disarmingly simple, once you know how. But it's working it out first that's the hard bit and I've cracked that, with a little help from Euclid, Galileo, Fermat, Leibniz, Newton, standing on the shoulder of giants and all that. There!* His chalking clicked to a final halt. *It's complete now.*

So?—I said. *It just looks like a very complex drawing on a wall to me.*

You think so?—he said, then bent over and stepped through it.

My heart must have skipped several beats. I ran around in circles, a headless chicken clucking to myself, saying really useful stuff like *oh shit this isn't happening, this can't be happening.*

Then a hand came back out of the wall, pulled a few chalk lines aside then Malthrop stepped out again. The candlelight flickered and I stood there stunned, just listening to his breath and mine. *Aren't you coming with me then?*—he smiled amicably.

I felt almost tired now, defeated in my understanding of anything anymore. *Where to?*

Back to my house, where the main Machine is. This is a shortcut now, I have the same shape drawn on a wall in my house. Space has collapsed temporarily between the two points. I know, I've just been there and back.

I hesitated. *You know what I'm going to do next anyhow, right?*

He nodded his head. *I've put the kettle on.*

Nice touch, I sighed.

Did he drug the tea? Might have, I wouldn't have put it past him. Hard to say, I was in such an altered state anyway by the time he sat me into the cockpit of that weird Machine and strapped me in and pressed the button. I went back. Of course I did. Who wouldn't, out of morbid curiosity? A man like me with a ruined life like mine, with all the best bits behind him and nothing but foul-smelling shite staring him in the face up ahead. Surely I had nothing to lose?

I went back and stepped out of his Machine. There was no one around, I walked out of his house and made my way across London until I found my old flat. On the way I saw enough newspapers to know it was for real. I was back in time alright, Thatcher was still in power. People's clothes and models of cars, everything was different but strangely familiar, pretty much as I remembered it.

It was 8 am. I knocked on the door of his flat and he answered it. Him. Young, smarmy, full-of-himself me, turning his nose up at my smell. But I could tell he noticed our resemblance and didn't like it. The more I proved it and made it clear to him, the more I saw him crumple before my eyes. I was the strong one. I was the avenging angel of truth, a living revelation, while he was the frightened mortal backing away in cowardly terror.

There's a particular kind of cringing fear that's sickening to witness, it doesn't induce pity or compassion in an attacker, quite the opposite. Someone ought to school people in how to avoid those displays, they only encourage killers. Yes, that would be more use than any number of pepper sprays and rape alarms.

I knew he was weak and stupid, and that in his future he had already failed to learn his lesson, had already failed to stop himself from falling, from turning into the tramp and drunk I had become. At least, that's what I thought I knew. But that was the one lie Malthrop had told me, the one trick God plays on all of us, and it's his best one.

I thought I was strangling the younger me, to replace him with myself. As I drowned him head first in the bath, I was already planning to put his clothes on and start off to work as if nothing had happened. Do his day's piss-easy work, take his big fat pay-cheque, fuck his girlfriend silly. I thought I would make a better shot of his life this time around, learn from both our mistakes, never fall by the wayside and become a failure, a down-and-out again. But then I wouldn't have existed . . .

I was wrong. I was strangling myself as well as him. I was drowning both of us. When his body finally went limp beneath my hands, I watched it evaporate like steam in the early morning light, and then . . . my head went fuzzy.

Suddenly I couldn't remember how to play the stock market as clearly as I thought I had just a moment beforehand. I wasn't looking forward to seeing his girlfriend so much as worrying about what the hell to say to her and whether she would rumble I was an impostor.

I was a stranger in my own life again, with one hell of a sense of déjà vu. Fear and hopelessness descended over me. I felt as if I was a passenger in an aeroplane who had just murdered the captain while sleepwalking. I fell back and sat down and stared straight ahead, shocked.

My life was on autopilot, and I didn't know how to land.

You seriously expect me to believe a word of that?—Wroclaw asks.

Not at first, not right now . . . Wilbir smiles, *but I'm glad you taped it.*

I'm not, Wroclaw sighs. *This is a police station, not a science fiction writers' circle.*

Whatever, Wilbir grins. *But if you've just stumbled upon this guy Malthrop and his house and his Machine, then strange things are about to start happening to you. I guarantee it.*

Wroclaw stands and shakes his head. *You're the strangest, this week, buddy. Fish and chips?*

Vinegar and salt please, Wilbir replies, licking his lips.

Wroclaw never stops working. On his afternoon off he suddenly decides to phone an old contact at Huddersfield University, or *Huddersfield Polytechnic* as he still calls it.

Jason? It's Wroclaw here. Remember you built that model for me of the Wilson-Davies house for the high court trial?

Yes, of course I do.

I think I have another job for you. Something really big and strange. You might need a couple of technicians to help you out. We can fly you down and provide all the photographs you need if you can carry out a measured survey.

Sure, sounds interesting, sounds . . . major. What is it?

Hush hush, strictest confidence of course, but it's that so-called House Of Horrors in Camden that's just hit the news.

Oh yes, is that on your patch these days? Weren't you South London?

It's full of some weird machinery, Jason. But we think it actually works, that it's designed to do something. If you build a scale model from a survey then maybe you could test it, analyse it, retro-engineer it, or whatever the current buzzword is.

Sounds like a flaming flying-saucer, mate.

Not far off it, actually, but man-made, over many years, by some kind of nut job.

How big is this machine?

It fills the whole building, so that's about thirty feet long by ten across, twenty high.

There is a sudden scream from the living room and Wroclaw jumps out of his skin. *Hold on a minute, Jason, hold on. Tilda has just let out a shriek about something, I'm putting the phone down for a minute, I'll be back.*

Wroclaw dashes through to the living room to find Tilda on her knees on the floor, white-face, the television switched to mute by her for the first time in living memory, her hands shaking.

What is it? What's wrong?—Wroclaw asks, and her mouth opens and closes on words that refuse to form. He goes over and sits down beside her.

I just saw something, she whispers, out of breath, shivering. *I'm not going mad, but something just materialised on that table, right in front of me, then disappeared.*

What was it? Wroclaw asks, perplexed, eyes wide.

It was moving, whirring, light was coming out of it. You think I'm insane don't you?

No, no . . . Wroclaw breathes in, then goes and gets some paper, *Draw it . . . please, Tilda, here.*

Her shaking hands slowly sketch out intersecting wheels and cogs and pistons. *It was filled with yellow light coming from inside itself. It was shaking the table.*

How big?—Wroclaw asks, his heartbeat quickening, his head feeling faint.

The whole length of the table.

Wroclaw returns slowly to the phone in the hallway, carrying the sketch in his hand, like a wounded man, confused. *Jason?*

Wroclaw, you ok? Is Tilda ok? Nothing wrong there, I hope?

Everything's fine. Jason, don't worry about it. This model of this machine we were talking about . . . what scale do you think you would make it?

Up to you, old man, big as you like within reason. I'd have to see the original first of course, moving parts are hard to do the smaller they get. You tell me.

85

What if I didn't tell you, Jason? What scale would you make it then?
What a strange thing to say . . . let me see . . . one to ten I think.
And what size would that make the model?
Three feet long by two feet high of course.
Thanks, Jason.
What? Sorry?
That's exactly what we'll do, I'll be back in touch next week.

MECHAGNOSIS #07

~ *Suburban Séance* ~

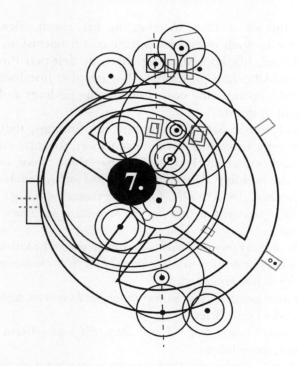

"Don't think I'm wooing you! Angel, even if I am you won't come for my call is always full of rising, you can't move against such a current, it's just too strong . . .
—Rainer Maria Rilke, from the *Duino Elegies*, #7.

Wroclaw throws a case meeting in his room. Bearing no resemblance to such occasions portrayed on television, there is no whiteboard, blackboard or flipchart, no felt-pen flow-charts nor pin-board bearing gruesome photographs. Just four people around a table, comparing notes and sharing findings and voicing theories and opinions.

The forensic pathologist tables his findings, that despite Wroclaw's early fears and media speculation, forensic and DNA analysis have conclusively revealed that there were only four bodies in the building. *Malthrop's mother and father, and Melanie and Mitchell Cheswick. The fifth DNA trace is presumed to be Scott Malthrop himself, who is presumed to have fled the premises a few hours before the police's arrival.*

Why so many presumptions?—Wroclaw wants to know.

Well there's a problem with Malthrop's DNA. We're having difficulty distinguishing it from his father's.

But what about all those missing tramps and winos we suspect him of killing?—Asks Lynn Brien.

You didn't believe that old guy's story, did you?—Brian Lindsay corrects her, incredulous.

Not at face value, but the interviews we conducted at the homeless hostels seemed to check out, you were there. That bit of Wilbir's story was true apparently . . .

Who's Wilbir?—The pathologist asks Wroclaw quietly.

William Birnam, a mysterious tramp . . . Wroclaw answers.

Well, Wroclaw clears his throat, raising his voice, *. . . sadly, and in fairness, those who sleep rough, dying in British winters, disappearing without trace, are hardly news, not necessarily news in itself at all.*

Which is why we thought Malthrop might be choosing them for his experiments: the ideal victims, guinea pigs.

But what experiments? We've just been told there's not a trace of these missing persons within the house. Surely you're not signing up for this sci-fi time-travel line? You've been reading too many comics, Brian.

Lynn Brien looks at him angrily.

Not you, Wroclaw sighs, *strictly Jane Austen for you, I know.*

Lynn frowns even more and sighs to herself, angrily.

We know he worked with acids, to render the skeletons he put into the machine. He could have disposed of any number of corpses, simply by using higher concentrations.

True? Wroclaw turns to the pathologist, who nods his head affirmatively.

Nonetheless we only have DNA for five individuals, four dead, one Malthrop himself, end of story, so we move on. Finding Malthrop, any ideas?

Draw up a conjectural life history for him to date.

Yes and get it out on television, Crimewatch, along with updated computer images of his appearance. Appeal for more information even, about his youth and childhood, information from people in the immediate area. We know he never strayed far from there.

So where is he now? Spain? South America?

Seems so unlikely for a man who's lived all his days in one place, less than a square mile, up to that point.

Not as unlikely as him still being here. What are you implying?

I know it's crazy, Wroclaw sighs, putting his big hands on the table, letting his eyes wander over their wrinkled backs as if searching there for clues. *But despite what we think, doesn't it feel as if he is still here somehow?*

Lynn Brien and Brian Lindsay talk quietly at the window later, after Wroclaw has left for the evening.

You know what I think? I think he sees that Crawford woman too often.

Carrie Crawford? Too often for what? Lynn asks absentmindedly, feigning interest in a paper she is reading.

You know . . . Brian says. *It's the oldest story in the book. I reckon he fancies her.*

Lynn lets out a deep guttural laugh and rolls her eyes up to meet his, turning a page. *You reckon?*

Yeah . . . Brian turns away.

He must be thirty years her senior . . . at least, Lynn says.

From looking through a gap in the blinds, one hand raised

to fidget, Brian turns back around. *Yeah, exactly, I didn't say it was mutual.*

Unrequited love of the bereaved girlfriend of a murder victim in a case you're in charge of . . . juicy. But she must invite him over . . . no way could he be making that many legitimate enquiries . . . you might be onto something . . .

Thanks.

Not the sort of puzzle we should be solving though is it?

No. Fancy a pint? Brian finds he has said this without even planning it, not even for a second.

This time Lynn has turned away, raking in a drawer, feigns disinterest, then answers: *Yeah, why not . . . gossip makes me thirsty.*

For more gossip . . . Brian laughs.

No! For white wine or cider. Why? You got more?

Wine or gossip? Dualities, dualities . . .

Dualities . . . Lynn repeats in her best Wroclaw accent, low and gruff, and they both laugh heartily, turning to leave and lock up.

Malthrop spins in wheels within wheels. Moving through the nineteen seventies, early youth, the golden time before responsibility. Of all the ages, the eras his life contains, this is the one he would like most to disappear into, become ultimately lost within perhaps, buried. Saturdays, going around shops with his mum, helping his dad in his workshop, proximity and understanding of the adult world, but not yet initiated into its vile burdens and humiliations. A kind of utopian view of society and its routines, but perhaps the true one, an insight we all lose later.

His father's tweed jacket falls from a chamber and is drawn across his face and nostrils: he inhales its tobacco aroma. The smell of black faux-leather car seats cooking in early summer sunshine. The languid bliss of long summer holidays. His mother's face: a light comes on within the cockpit and a collage of a hundred colour photographs shifts slowly across his field of view. Youthful, beautiful, smiling, returning home with shopping bags, excitement of some forgotten occasion . . . what could it have been? Prize-giving, graduation? It drifts, fades into a pleasant uncertainty, a miasma of warmth and well-being.

Further back, further. Summer evenings, playing alone, alone. Cycling around their little backyard, this giving him remarkable pleasure. His childhood bicycle, complete with stabilisers, enters the chamber on an overhead rail, its wheels spinning, blades of blue light flickering through its spokes, to the soundtrack of the local ice cream van.

His friend Vince's dog: the pelt of a spaniel wet with rain falls across him, then his cousin's Shetland Collie, a decade-specific breed (have they since died out?). Chopper bikes and Artex plaster. Chilli con carne served in orange Tupperware. In the Artex chamber the touch receptors in his hands and face brush over length after length of sharp plaster like frozen storm-tossed oceans. The aroma of too much fried cooking burnt into its atomic structure.

His parents' voices echoing in rooms of dark polished wood. The smell of wood-polish blows into the cockpit. The sound of a teapot clinking on china. Open windows, late traffic. Twittering of summer evening birds.

Just as well it is summer now. The air is so pleasant, the late evening hour so interminably languid and dreamy, a welcome cool after a day of claustrophobic urban heat.

Seralta and Merkiel are part of the walls now, fused with the concrete, white as powder, only their nose and mouths and ears occasionally surface imperceptibly, to reach out beyond their tomb. They each stand upright within the walls, like buried statues, sentinels, guardians, glued within the fabric of Scott Malthrop's house, enshrined.

The sun falling on the concrete all day warms them, and their eyes roll closed in contentment and forgetfulness, occasionally reaching out hands in their sleep, finding each other's fingertips.

Could passers-by below ever see or imagine them? Only as momentary phantoms, optical illusions, rain-stain patterns evaporating within the hour. All buildings were once alive, incomplete, at the time of their birth. All buildings sleep, dreaming of us, their first lovers.

Something stirs the angels. Like a door thrown open somewhere, a sudden time-breeze blows over them and draws them inward and backward like a vortex of voices, twisted and burnt.

Like wires or ropes, entwining, they whine, actuate, fluctuate. Gathered together, funnelled, transported and spat-out, they find themselves in the darkened church of Scott Malthrop senior.

The tramps and down-and-outs sit marvelling in the pews at the sight of a strange light-emitting machine before the altar. Some of them fall to their knees and cross themselves.

In the shafts of coloured sunlight from the stained-glass windows, the angels materialise, become momentarily visible, change into smoke and mist then change back again then turn around, spin, flicker. The stones of the rose window itself almost seem to swell and rotate, stone and mortar shifting, spray of sand and dust, as if the church itself is a living organ, the window its beating heart or palpitating lung, muscles spasming, clutching, unclutching. The window rotates and expands and contracts, a focussing eye, a camera lens, a cosmic vagina: taking life in and out.

Seralta is drawn down helplessly towards the machine as it spins faster, then is drawn in sideways, all her dimensions compressed to zero. In panic, Merkiel thrusts himself into the skull of one of the drunks and makes him scream and babble like a madman, speaking in tongues, until the others hold him down. Unable to move the body any longer: he has no choice but to exit, slithering onto the floor like black oil, then driven irrevocably up towards the spinning wheels. He cries out but his voice becomes bells trilling at infinite pitch, momentarily, in every belfry in each town in every nation, the music of accelerated time. Everything becomes white light and speed. He finds Seralta again, his only wish.

Out of the pure yellow light, a glowing chandelier, extinguished, the angels descend. It is a suburban séance, six or seven pairs of hands around a circular table. Only the hands are visible. Seralta

92

and Merkiel swirl around like candle-smoke or evening fog, traffic smog, looking for the lips that make the voices they now hear passing through them, shaking them like earthquakes. *Carrie. Mitch.* The face and eyes emerge, a scream, blood-curdling. All hands holding. An old woman at the head of the table, eyelids flickering. *Mitch,* the voice says, and Carrie's face clears the mist around it. *Mitch . . . do you know? Do you realise?* Seralta and Merkiel become white snakes and vanish into each ear of the old woman, driving her mad. They lift a lit candle and hurl it across the table in rage. Inside the head of the old woman on the floor as the others gather around, trying to revive her, Merkiel makes her tongue wag, spouting nonsense, until he sees the beloved face of Carrie rising towards him out of the darkness. He weeps, he makes her weep, he lifts himself as if to kiss her, he vanishes into her eyes like the wave of an endless ocean. He enters her dreams.

Merkiel disassembles in the sleeping mind of Carrie, becomes insubstantial as her breath, a mist upon her mirror. Carried on the wings of a shrieking owl, unblinking, he crosses ten neighbourhoods then finds himself spewed out like a half-heard word into the room of Wroclaw, through an open summer window.

Something in the face, a previous template, unreachable memory, makes him fall over it like a predator's wings, a dust sheet falling over a forgotten chair. He mops Wroclaw's brow, wipes the grey hair from his eyes and whispers into his ears:

PUT BACK THE FOURTH FLY WHEEL.

Wroclaw wakes up with a shout and wakes up Tilda. This is unfortunate, spoiling as it does, one of the rare recent occasions of them sleeping together.

What is it dear, what is it? Tilda asks, alarmed, peering into his eyes like those of a madman. *You were talking about wheels . . . wheels . . .*—she prompts him.

Yes, he whispers to himself, pulling himself together, *the fourth fly wheel.*

What does that mean?

Beats me . . . He stands up and shrugs, *. . . dream talk, crazy talk . . .* and goes to the bathroom to wash his face.

Catching sight of himself in the mirror, he pauses and looks into his own eyes, thinking. He returns to the bedroom and sees Tilda is already sleeping again, snoring lightly. He turns back to the living room and sits down at the dining table to admire his working model of Malthrop's Machine.

He runs his hand absent-mindedly, then with increasing focus, over various cogs and wheels, trying to analyse the small areas of linked motion he has managed to get going.

What's missing from you, my little beauty, eh? He murmurs. *Do you even have a fly wheel, a fourth fly wheel, a fourth anything? What makes you tick? Why won't you work for me?*

Carrie Crawford opens the door to Wroclaw and greets him with her now familiar diminutive: *It's you . . .* She retires to the living room, leaving him to close the door himself.

How are we doing? He asks, imaginatively, leafing through one of her magazines, while she lights herself a cigarette by the window, drawing the curtains.

Oh . . . coping . . . she says, turning around, arms folded.

He lifts his eyes to catch her expression, and she smiles imperceptibly.

Without saying so, they both gravitate towards the armchair and settee and sit perpendicular to each other, staring more straight ahead than at one other.

Funny you talking about the nightmares you had at first, gradually passing, over the last six months.

Funny, how? Carrie grimaces, crossing her legs.

Not funny, strange, I mean.

Why?

Because I've started getting them now . . .

Carrie laughs, throwing her head back, and Wroclaw beams like a child to see this. *Are you serious?*

Oh yeah. I wish I wasn't. Weird stuff, about Malthrop, even though I never met the guy, and about his weird machine.

So maybe your wife was right about not letting that scale model into the house . . .

It's just a model, Wroclaw shakes his head.

D'you really think so? You seem spooked.

Wroclaw shivers and shakes himself and sits up at this remark, suddenly insulted and self-conscious.

Carrie sighs: *now who's counselling who, eh?* She gets up and pours him a drink and brings it over to him, leans down and kisses him on the forehead.

He feels startled and a little embarrassed by this, so changes the subject: *How was your second week back at work by the way, still awkward?*

No . . . it's getting better, Carrie says, sitting on the arm of the sofa. *It's probably in my head, the feeling of everyone talking about me afterwards, looking at me like a freak, treating me differently, I probably imagine it . . .*

Probably not actually, Wroclaw frowns. *Nietzsche said "there is something terrible about people to whom something terrible has happened . . ."*

God! That's horrible, did he really say that? He was the nazi guy, wasn't he?

No, Carrie, not at all. He was just seized upon and misrepresented by the nazis, he was dead by the time they came around. But he did say it, and disturbing though it is, it holds some water.

Mmm . . . Carrie purrs. *Is it reversible? Will I get less terrible, as my terrible loss recedes into the past?*

Do you want it to?

I just want to be normal, you know that, I'm still young, not like . . .

Not like an old fuck-up like me, eh?

Carrie smiles and puts her glass down, kneels on the floor next to his chair, reaches her hand out as if to stroke his hair. *You've aged nicely, old man, worn your scars and wrinkles well, like a fine old map of the world.*

Wroclaw nods. *Yes, I suppose that's the trick, isn't it?—Not to try to remain unblemished, but to add all our hurts and shocks into our make-up, our skin, to grow with our experiences.*

Are you sure you didn't train as a psychiatrist? Carrie asks, lifting a lovely hand to run through her long hair, eyeing him strangely.

Bit of psychology in the training, obviously, but not as such.

What's the difference, anyway?

Psychology and Psychiatry? Theoretical and applied, I suppose.

Ahh, of course. Never really been a hands-on man, have you?

How d'you mean? Wroclaw scratches his head, sipping his whisky.

You know, a thinker, abstract. You're like a chess master, Wroclaw. And what are you?

Carrie suddenly laughs loudly and stands up and strolls away across the room. *An Olympic javelin-thrower,* she says and mimes, in macho gestures, arms raised, legs braced.

Golly . . . Wroclaw says drily, and hides behind another sip of his drink, sheepish.

That's why I like you. We're so different. You're like I wish my dad had been. I was always too clever for him. He couldn't handle a clever girl I think, probably why I had to leave home.

You're too clever for me too, Carrie. Wroclaw laughs, and her eyes widen. *When you solve mysteries all day, you learn to value the unravellable* . . .

Sir, Lynn Brien enters Wroclaw's office without knocking and puts the local paper and a couple of internet print-outs on his desk. *We have a problem that won't go away.*

Yes? Wroclaw looks up.

The Malthrop case. Ghouls and over-eager reporters, trophy hunters, pseudo-scientists, freaks of all kinds . . . . *They keep trying to break into the house at Clevedane Lane, tampering with the locks and windows. We need a permanent solution.*

What do you suggest?

Concrete the whole thing . . . Brian Lindsay says, following her into the room. *Seriously, my cousin is a builder, I could get a quote for shuttering the whole thing and pouring concrete in from above. They have lorries you hire that just turn up and pump the stuff out like petrol. Seal the entire building over, take the plywood sheets away once it's set, job done.*

But it's a crime scene.

Is it? An unsolved crime scene, let's face it. Four years old. Forensics have everything they need. You even have your beloved scale model, which you can bequeath to the British Museum upon your death, sorry, a little

96

joke there. Anyway. Yes. Concrete it. End of story. They demolished Fred and Rosemary West's house, you know, and the house of that janitor bloke, Huntley, the one who killed the little girls.

Wroclaw nods. *Alright, get a quote. We'll show it to the superintendent.*

Did I tell you I went to a séance, by the way? Carrie suddenly asks out of the blue.

No. Wroclaw frowns. *You're kidding.*

I just knew you'd say that, you old cynic. No. I did, and it was very interesting and strange . . . . Strange in a good way.

You believe in all that stuff?

No, I didn't. But I'm open-minded. More so than you, I'm presuming by your expression. But yes . . . it wasn't a fraud, I would say.

You made contact? Wroclaw tries to keep the sarcasm out of his voice but isn't sure if he succeeds.

With Mitch, Yes, I think so. Yes, it gave me a great sense of peace afterwards, very comforting. The Medium said . . . you don't believe in any of this, do you?

Wroclaw opens his palms in a gesture of evenness.

She said Mitch and Melanie are together now, in some kind of limbo, and they want to find peace, to say goodbye to those they loved.

Wroclaw tilts his head, silently, respectfully, deep in thought.

Before Wroclaw leaves, while Carrie is at the toilet, he notices her photo albums on her shelf. She has shown them to him before, and his fascination makes him feel a little queasy. He takes his favourite down and flicks through it. Somehow, he gets so drawn in that he forgets to put it away before she comes back. He discovers she is standing next to him, but is relieved to see she seems fascinated rather than insulted by his intrusion.

The past is weird isn't it?

Wroclaw nods silently.

I wish I was older, Carrie sighs.

Wroclaw looks up at her in surprise.

Or you were younger. Why do you think, silly, she punches his arm. *We could have been contemporaries,* she rolls every letter in the word, *or even an item. Wild, but it's what you're thinking too, or feeling it*

97

at least, if you can admit it to yourself.

Yes, Wroclaw sighs, shivering. *Time travel would have a certain appeal wouldn't it?—If it were possible?*

Oh, it's possible, Carrie says, as they move towards the door and he puts his coat on. *We're all time-travelling forwards right now, just by living, if you think about it... and going back by remembering. Only problem is just that no one's ever found the brakes, the speed control, or the full reverse gear.*

Or even the key . . . Wroclaw finishes her sentence a minute later, outside in his car, talking quietly to himself, feeling as if some enormous penny is about to drop inside the slot machine of his head. *Or the key . . .* He whispers.

Jason?

Wroclaw.

The model you made me. Is it possible that something is missing from it?—That something was missing from the crime scene, from the full-scale Machine? I know you said it was probably just an irrational pile of old junk, but could you analyse it, using geometry or the laws of dynamics or something, and then ask what might need to be added to it to complete it?

An occupant.

Sorry?

I had similar thoughts myself, a few weeks ago. I meant to phone you. There were several control areas in the Machine, as if a human being was supposed to stand or sit there.

Are you going to tell me I should put some pet gerbils in this thing?!

Nice idea, but no. I was thinking lemons might be about the right size.

Lemmings? Don't jerk me around, Jason.

Lemons, you deaf old goat, as in oranges and lemons and the bells of saint Clemens. They're about the right size for the scale of the model, and the acid inside them would electrolyse in a way not unlike the electromagnetic field of the human body. Stick a nail in either side of it, you know, like . . .

Like the old high school experiment, I remember. How to make a primitive battery, a light bulb, run a wire between the two nails and it lights up. Bingo.

That's it, Wroclaw. Sounds crazy, I know, but I think it might bridge the gaps in whatever crazy circuit that guy was trying to set up. Let me know how you get on.

Don't worry, I will, Jason. Thanks again. I will . . .

MECHAGNOSIS #08

~ *Concrete Coffin* ~

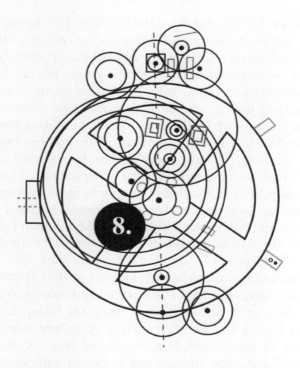

"*My call is a an outstretched arm and its high, reaching open hand is always before you, open incomprehensible being, wide open to defend and warn off...*"
—Rainer Maria Rilke, from the *Duino Elegies*, #7.

Late summer. Malthrop drifts in the Machine. He's never stayed in this long before. Becalmed, lost sideways out of time, a thousand sunsets blind his eyes, pulsing like a heartbeat. Evening birdsong, childhood memories of holidays, swaying pines filtering blades of yellow light on dusty farm tracks. Flies rising up into the air from mirror-still mill ponds. Sounds of distances, peacefulness.

His memory of Melanie rests inside him like a timid dove, black hair like his mother's, ruffled by an evening breeze. He sees her speaking, dancing, spinning him in a circle but he can no longer make out her words. What is happening to him? He is falling, fading, like old Polaroid photographs in a forgotten drawer. He is decaying, maturing, evolving into some essence of longing, dissolved in air. Falling like a leaf, tolling like a church bell.

Has the Machine broken finally? Or is he broken? He begins to see glimpses beyond his customary cage. Like sprocket holes in rewinding film, flickering vignettes of the city around him play through him, over him, as surprising and refreshing as spring rain. He feels as if the Machine is rising up, taking him higher somehow, like an ascending aircraft, offering him strange views of the city as living metaphor, outside of time. A vast library, repository for the lost dreams and hopes of unknowable lives. But not lost. He has it now, the key, access to all of it, a psychic librarian. Is he dying he wonders?

Wroclaw is at home, reading over an extract of Malthrop's diary that has been recovered from Clevedane Lane:

Malthrop's Notes on the Workshopping of Fat Old Bald Men

My theory is that civilisation is some kind of parabolic curve on a graph chart. On the way up, a society will worship its elders, hence our Victorian parks filled with statues of fat

102

old bald men. On the way down, after the tipping-point, youth-worship will kick in. Those fat old bald men were great philosophers, physicists, philanthropists, people of enormous learning but often laughable physical appearance. It takes a great deal of time to learn anything worth passing on. But today our heroes, by way of contrast, are of course footballers, television chefs, celebrity gardeners, singers who don't write their own songs. But they all have youth and beauty. The problem is, we have nothing to learn from youth and beauty, nothing to gain from its worship other than jealousy and lust. From the fat old bald men, we might have learned to further unlock the atom, explore the stars, build new empires of the mind. But no. Today we regress like children in front of our television sets every night, slobbering like asylum patients, fixated on the surface, the shallow, the short-term, the physical. We retreat, each into our own corners, to masturbate feverishly while our intelligence dies of neglect.

When we came to old age, or even middle-age, in a former era, we might have enjoyed respect, acclaim for our achievements. Today as we each approach this state, all we taste is the incoming sea of self-loathing. The prospect of being eaten alive by dogs, the younger bucks in our pack dragging down the sagging flesh. The end is not pretty. The law of the jungle.

Every year, a younger prime minister, a younger president, a younger role model. Time is running in reverse. All this is the signature of the far side of the parabolic curve. Remember its shape, remember its acceleration, after the turnaround. The only way is down.

Does this youth-worship explain our worship of machines?—Because machines are inorganic, un-ageing, the ultimate opposite of incontinent old men?

And has this youth-worship been transferred even into the machines themselves? So that old machines must be cast out too?—The new machines perpetually sought

103

out and worshipped?

Our culture has become focussed into a kind of theoretical-infinite acceleration: ultra-new, ultra-temporary, ultra-throwaway. As if such a philosophy could deliver rapid progress, light-speed development. But the opposite is true. Development depends on the consolidation of knowledge, not its perpetual loss, not on constant rediscovery of the wheel. The daily wasting of resources inherent in our obsessive way of life slows down our progress, like accumulating rust. The huge turning machine of our society, haemorrhaging fuel, will gradually slow and buckle, and grind to a creaking halt. Some future native will find our wreckage in the long grass and wonder what we were for. Why then do we share the mass-illusion of speeding up, while actually slowing? Are we clutching to some flywheel of the mind, broken loose, disengaged from the engine?

We have hypnotised ourselves into the global delusion that we are hurtling ever faster into our ever brighter future. In fact, we are running on the spot, on a treadmill disconnected from the cogwheels surrounding it, the forgotten apparatus of the civilisation of our fathers. Their machine might have carried us forwards, but no one alive remembers how to find the controls . . .

Wroclaw scratches his head and looks up absent-mindedly, while Tilda hoovers loudly all around him. *Did you throw that lemon away?*

What, dear?

Wroclaw shouts over the hoover noise: *That lemon! The one that was sitting in the model machine . . . I told you not to throw it in the bin.*

I didn't . . . Tilda replies but Wroclaw fails to hear her correctly. *I don't care if it was getting old. It wasn't mouldy. I asked you not to throw that bloody lemon away . . .* he trails off, his last few words hanging, shouted across the room as the hoover sound dies rapidly away.

Tilda has stopped, paused, looking at him, wide-eyed, mouth-open, furious. *Look. I didn't throw your damned smelly old lemon away, OK? I bloody didn't, you crazy old grump, so cut it out!*

Sorry—he backs down, timid again without the aural camouflage of hoover noise. *It's just you put things away so often that I lose trust in everything, myself, everything around me in this house. There's always this doubt in my head that whatever I might want and wherever I might think I put it last, you might have hidden it somewhere different without my consent.*

Consent? Tilda looks up from feather-dusting the fireplace, incredulous. *What do you think this is, the Czar's Winter Palace? Somebody has to keep this place tidy or you'd turn it into a bomb-site inside a week. Here . . .* She throws him the hoover, nearly bruising his head, knocking off his reading-glasses. *Clean the bloody house yourself for a change. I'm away out for a walk.*

Wroclaw is astounded this time. Such physically demonstrative rage is wildly out of character. She pauses at the door, putting her coat on . . . *AND THAT'S WITHOUT YOUR CONSENT!* -She yells and slams the door behind her.

Wroclaw is left staring straight ahead in shock, muttering to himself until he finds he is saying: . . . *the lemon . . . you didn't throw out the lemon . . . she didn't throw out the lemon . . . wait a minute.*

He stands up excitedly and paces over to the scale model Machine where it sits on the coffee table. *My God . . . if she didn't throw it out then that means . . .* he lifts his hand and puts his fingers forward in awe, into the central chamber where he saw the lemon sitting just two hours beforehand.

He gets up and empties the bins excitedly, to make sure. No thrown-away lemons. *My God . . . the hoover . . . the hoover . . . of course . . . wind. The fourth flywheel is the fourth element: wind. Malthrop's Machine was fed by the vents on the roof! Tilda! You're a genius! Come back so I can kiss you!* Wroclaw jumps up and runs to the front door and nearly runs down the street after her until it dawns on him he is still in his dressing-gown and slippers. Mrs Dawson over the road is out on her doorstep talking to the postman, and eyes him suspiciously and nervously, frowning, until he backs away in surrender, head bowed in submission, closing the door behind him.

He returns to the scale model in the living room and kneels down before it in respect, as if praying at an occult altar.

A bright sunlit day, soon to be baking hot. Why has it always been such days in Wroclaw's life when he chooses to wound himself? His heart is a-flutter as he gets out of his car outside Carrie Crawford's house, clutching flowers. Oh you old fool, he tells himself in vain, but the success with the miniature Machine has done something to him, adjusted him, recalibrated. Like a moth or Icarus, he feels himself climbing blindly towards the sun but is unable to do anything to stop. Pheromones, organic magnetism, destiny, fate, he runs on rails. He is helpless, and yet strangely empowered. He rings her doorbell.

Carrie sees the blurred figure through her frosted glass door, a clutch of colour at its waist. Oh no, she thinks. Not flowers. Not Wroclaw.

Something is wrong from the moment she opens the door. They both know it. But only Wroclaw is culpable, responsible for a course of action he has the option to abandon, divert, but is somehow unable to do so. The moment is locked on rails, horrible.

Hi. I brought you . . .

Her eyes widen, an eyebrow arching higher still. *So I see . . .*

She is turning away already, there has been no kiss. Only a brief perfunctory embrace, a misalignment of gestures, a tacit detachment, a non-meeting of eyes. His heart climbs and spins into its hopeless spirals, a coiled spring, a lark ascending, stalked by a bird of prey, a hawk.

Carrie, he says, and they face each other in the living room but her eyes are set hard and glassy, turned off to the right, like a doll's, staring off through the windows to some other reality.

Carrie, he repeats again, and the eyes turn to him but their expression is terrible, heartsick, derisory, contemptuous, loaded with disgust.

The phone rings. Saved by the bell. She walks to the hallway and her back is turned. Her face mostly invisible, part obscured while she talks, in a maze of mirror and occluded glimpses, refracted lines of sight.

Yes, uh-huh. Hi, George. Yes, I know . . .

This is a mistake, a mistake . . . a voice screams inside Wroclaw.

106

Leave, run, go . . .

Instead, he sits down, feeling light-headed, as if his legs have given way under him. He finds a sweat is running on his forehead, but why? Is it still that warm outside? Did he run from the car up the steps? He opens his hands to cool down and spreads his palms on the chair-rest, the table next to him. He finds his fingers resting on Carrie's diary, open, in progress, the ink still wet, her still talking in the hall.

He knows he shouldn't. He picks it up, turns the pages, and reads:

> Oh God. Don't tell me that old fool actually fancies me. I couldn't bear that. The embarrassment. The ignominy, there's a good word. Are men always so silly, no matter their age? When then does wisdom arrive? Indefinitely postponed. Not in this life but in the next one? Is it their pricks I wonder, that always make such fools of them? Oh I know, I know. What with our hormones and hot flushes and PMT, can we really be said to be any better? But at least in childbirth, child-rearing, there is something practical, simple, worthwhile. But in men, with their perpetual urge to lose their juice, there is somehow always some misconception (excuse the pun) that this activity reflects well on them, that it compliments their ego, that it's some kind of achievement. Holy smoke. To carry a baby for nine months is a physical endurance test, but to conceive one is certainly not. If they could fuck without their ego involved, we might forgive them all manner of other transgressions. Even their feverish thirst for infidelities might not be so revolting, were it not also caught up with some vague form of self-aggrandisement, some myth of freedom, escape from marital imprisonment. What tosh.

Carrie has re-entered the room, the telephone conversation finished. Somehow, Wroclaw hasn't noticed, having become so caught up in, horrified by, what he is reading.

That's my diary . . . Carrie says simply, mechanically, standing at the doorway from the hall, her face a pale mask.

I'm ... I'm ... sorry ... Wroclaw starts to say, as amazed and perplexed as anyone else by his own actions. With a start, he catches sight of himself in one of the hall mirrors and realises the flowers are still wrapped and lying on the table by his right hand, his left resting on the diary.

I want you to leave ... Carrie says quietly. And the air itself recoils at the words, freezes like a fog, releasing a precipitate of icy rain, a thousand falling daggers. His eyes water, his mouth opens, wordless. He feels like a landed fish, floundering. The atmosphere is unbreathable. He stands up.

I'll call you ... he says lamely, automatically, as they pass like marionettes on rails in the hallway, as she reaches for the door. And she doesn't even say don't. Doesn't say anything at all.

Wroclaw drives around town for about an hour before it dawns on him that he doesn't know where he is going, and only then it's just because he finds himself about to take a turn that might bring him back into Carrie's street again.

He looks at the sky, waiting at the traffic-lights, autumn sun beating down like a merciless eye, swaying, mocking him, the first leaves falling. He changes course, he heads downtown, still not sure where he's going. But deep down, deep, he knows, he knows. His favourite drinking haunts, dark, anonymous. Eternal Saturdays, he wants to lose himself in the blur. Is this the meaning of loneliness?—subconscious request by the disheartened drone to be re-absorbed into the hive? But where is the signpost, the Queen Bee? What other species on earth has so little idea of what it actually is?—despite all its tools and evidence. Evidence. And him a detective. But after all these years all he has ever done is amass facts. But what use are facts in themselves? He may have proven repeatedly who did what sordid thing to who when, but why? The motive, the real motives ... something we just pretend is clear-cut. In crimes of anger, domestics, quickly regretted, tragedies, perhaps. But the calculation, the cold-blooded ... the warped and deranged. No, there's never any answer there, unless you want to buy into evil. Or is that only a label, a catch-all?

No. He turns into a sidestreet. Evil is what he feels now, this sickness in his stomach, this perversity, an urge to cancel badness with more badness, to out-bad God and reality, to shock it all and oneself back into a state of passion, from one of unbearable numbness and boredom. To regain control, to make God, or humanity at least, sit up and listen.

He parks his car absent-mindedly, then wakes up as he walks away, realising where his route is going to take him past. His footsteps slow down, hesitantly, admiringly, as he looks up at the house of Scott Malthrop, now encased in smooth concrete. There is something mute and smooth and immaculate about it now, like a sleeping face, eyes closed. But whose?

He shivers as he passes, and feels somehow compelled to cross the street and run his hand across its window sill and door frame, sealed forever, sexless, declined. But not like a tomb, no, he shakes his head as he moves away, looking over his shoulder. No. More like a power-station, electrical sub-station, a transformer. Out-of-bounds, something hidden and dangerous, but mysteriously essential. Danger Of Death. Keep Out. Trespassers Prosecuted.

In the darkened hush of The King's Arms, Wroclaw pulls up a pew and begins a night's bout. He feels like a chess master, a saloon gunslinger, settling down for a duel, man-to-man. But with who? No. Man to bar, man to existential angst. Yes, that's it. He's taking the bar on. A one man contest with reality, with drinks as the stakes, the chips. He knows himself, the context is heroic, despite or perhaps because of, the dice being loaded, the corrupt house of God having rigged the tables, defeat being inevitable. The struggle gladiatorial, of David and Goliath.

Everyone else, those not locked in a struggle of their own and equally lost, see of course, that he is not heroic, only pitiful. Whisky, gin, rum, vodka. He varies the diet. Think of it as an experiment. Controlled conditions. Looking for the key. The magical mixture of poison elixirs to carry him over, to bring back his youth, his pride, his self-respect. To give him Malthrop, Malthrop's head on a plate, mystery solved, case closed. To bring him . . . Carrie. Carrie. Oh how women's names become musical, time and again, coming and going like a tide of sighs. Carrie's gratitude and love, admiration. You solved it. You brought Mitch back. You brought shit back. You solved nothing. Failure.

The room is distorting. When he goes to the toilet he feels the chequerboard floor accelerating past him, the walls tilting. Things aren't staying still any longer. Meanings shift. The smiling girls at the nearest table seem to be looking at him in a way, like somebody famous, fabulous, a caged beast. No, you're not walking steady anyway. Stare straight ahead. Focus on the fantasy, the beautiful dream of it all, the face unmet, the words as yet unspoken, the chase, the thrill, the sad and melancholy waste of it all. All the days and hours that gurgle down our gutters. Dear God. Voyage forward, into the mirrors behind the bar, outside of time, beyond the constrictions of this hair-shirt present. Go beyond. Into the heart of it all. Shatter reality. He lifts his glass. He thinks about . . . a filmic cliché: to launch the glass forward and shatter the mirror behind the bar and see all the humdrum fragments of himself released, all bad, all laughing, glass falling down to reveal the dark netherworld beyond: giant maggots and lice and spiders feeling their way out to crawl up and down, outwards in every direction across the freeze-frame present, soiling a world of torn photographs.

But no, someone is touching his arm, talking into his ear. He starts, almost recoiling in fear, he struggles to make his eyes focus, steady his voice into a coherent tone in response.

Hey, you're that copper, ain't you?

Wroclaw finds he is shaking his head, but saying yes. Irrational.

You still looking for that Malthrop character?

I'm off duty . . . Wroclaw murmurs.

Yeah, me too . . . the bloke laughs hoarsely, *I'm just a tramp nine to five to impress the tourists.*

Wroclaw pulls his vision into focus and sees the apparition in front of him. His clothes are indeed torn, long white hair, a down-and-out. For a moment he has the fabulous delusion that his new companion is not visible in the mirror, or is someone else, a respectable middle-aged lady in a white fur coat talking about a west-end play.

You've been looking in the wrong places, copper.

How do you mean? Who are you, anyway?

Who are you?—More to the point. If you want to find Malthrop, you have to find yourself. That's the deal he peddles . . .

Deals. Wroclaw snorts. *I don't do deals,* he says, enjoying the macho sound of it, throwing his whisky back, looking straight ahead again.

He ain't never left, mate . . . one last sentence pours into his ears before he sees a flash of darting silver in the mirror, the old white-haired weasel high-tailing it out the bar.

Wroclaw puts his glass down and feels strangely sober all of a sudden. The barman catches his eye for a moment, for a change. *Was that a ghost or could you see him too?*—Wroclaw asks, smiling stupidly, attempting a joke, but the words come out revealingly slurry.

You think you might've had too many, guv'nor?

Frustrated, Wroclaw realises this response doesn't answer his question. *But did you?*—He asks but the barman's shoulder is turning away. *Did you see him?* He finds he has raised his voice now, in anger, people starting to look at him. He is no longer in the same reality as them. He is in his own stream, a timeline, the interactions between his and theirs occasional, fraught with danger and misunderstanding. He stands up and staggers out.

It's not as late as he thought. Still light in fact. Red sunset sky, the bustling crowds all turned to black silhouettes, shadow men and women, cut-outs in a morality play. The Decameron. Punch and Judy. He pushes through them, thinking he catches sight of the old tramp up ahead. He feels like he is swimming through mud, people bumping into him, cursing him. Winded, he cries out in desperation. He wants to get ahead, to catch up with the old grey weasel, to find an answer. Colliding again, he falls, and people step over him, trample him, kick, curse. He rolls into the gutter. A bus whizzes by, tooting its horn. He hears a police siren, and he picks himself up and hides in the crowds again, hurrying on, feeling all their eyes on him like pinpricks of fire, hot black kisses, bites. He is cold and wet suddenly. He finds blood on his forehead, mud on his trousers. He staggers

111

with the crowd then is bounced, as if by an eddy in a stream, an urban pedestrian current, spinning off into an alleyway leading to a church. He slows down, disbelieving, as if moving in a dream. The open door of the church gapes like a glowing orange mouth. Salvation Army women are handing out soup in bowls with ladles from large metallic vats.

He walks towards them slowly, as if sleepwalking, half planning to produce his ID and interview them, but they look him up and down once, calmly, and hand him some soup. He tries to protest, then laughs, grasping the irony, looking down at the stains and rips on his clothes, then realises it shouldn't be funny. They bustle him forward, following the others into the church nave to where hymns are being sung, the down-and-outs gathered around in the hard pews, soup and breath smoking, steam unwinding heavenwards, merging with the atmosphere of stained glass and incense, wrapped in their duffle coats in the church's chill interior, in various stages of boredom and religious rapture.

Sitting in the pews, shoulder to shoulder with the indigent, Wroclaw laughs to himself again, the irony, then realises he can think of no one to whom he could tell this joke, who would not recoil in anger, pity and disgust at the context of his story. This makes him laugh even more, and he settles into his buttoned-up tattered raincoat, the warm glow of whisky still spreading inside him like an inverted tree, a glorious virus unpicking his insides, disassembling him, reassembling him into something bigger and better. Old and useless and written-off and dying, he smiles to himself in bittersweet self-pity, but turning into something dirty and forgotten underground: a protuberance, a distortion on the roots of life, a tuber, potato . . . raw material for vodka, firewater, engine fuel. I will burn again and again.

Then he finds his eyes have been watching something, resting on it, like underwater currents drawn around a stone, a buried tree stump. There, off to the left behind the altar: he can see geometric lines drawn on a wall, faintly, as if scrubbed over, erased, but still there, ghostly traces. He stands up as the hymn ends and makes his way over to look at the wall. He kneels, sits almost reverently in front of it and runs his hands over the marks. *My God* . . . he whispers . . . *what if Wilbir was telling the truth* . . .

112

Again, a voice, a figure, suddenly appears close to his left side, makes him jump and shiver. A young woman in Salvation Army costume, no looker, plumply smiling down at him with something uncertain in her eyes. His vision is clearing again, he feels steadier. *God . . . you mentioned God,* -she says softly. *I overheard you. He waits patiently for all of us. He will find you if you look for him.*

Yes . . . Wroclaw says, standing up, brushing himself down, . . . *that's what worries me.*

Wroclaw staggers back into his house at midnight, and Tilda gets out her bed specially to berate him. *What's got into you? What do you think you're playing at staggering in like this in this state? Do you have any idea the mess I found this house in when I got back this afternoon? Bin emptied all over the kitchen floor. What's all that about? Are you trying to drive me away? Trying to turn into an animal?—Like you're a wild dog in a cave? What are you trying to prove to the world? And what's this obsession with bloody lemons? Do you know I found ten rotten lemons lying around the living room last week . . .*

You what?

Lemons. They were all over the living room, in different corners like you'd been playing table tennis with them or something . . .

Why didn't you tell me about this at the time?

What? Are you crazy? That was the weekend I went to my mother's in protest, that was why. What are you ranting about now?

I've only ever bought four lemons, Tilda, for the experiment. That means the other ones are from the future.

What!? You're Nuts!

Me? You're the one who saw that fucking machine materialise in front of you before it had even been built. I wish I'd seen that . . .

Nonsense. That must just have been a trick of the light or something, I told you . . .

Don't you get it?!—Wroclaw suddenly roars at her and backs her up against a wall. *You only believe what people tell you. What you see on the frigging TV. You don't even believe your own eyes, and you don't use your fucking mind. Why don't you think for yourself anymore, Tilda?*

How dare you shout and swear at me! You're steaming drunk, and violent with it now. You're a disgrace!

113

If some newsreader on that telly, if Oprah Fucking Winfrey told you two and two made five tomorrow, you'd believe that completely, but if a flying saucer or a time machine lands on your flaming coffee table then you blank it. That's the pathetic state of your sensory perception, of your cognitive abilities, of your freewill and reason. That's what our culture has brought you to, has brought us all to. You're asleep, one of an army of sleepwalkers marching off a cliff. You're all so hypnotised you can't feel anything anymore, Couldn't feel a needle if I ran one right through your hand, while that damned television is on.

Tilda, shaking, speaks more quietly suddenly, into the shocked silence, afraid the neighbours might be listening. *I don't know you anymore, George. I don't have the slightest clue what you're talking about and I don't know you anymore.*

Of course you don't. You don't know yourself anymore. You've become your own unsolved mystery. You're a mollusc, an invertebrate . . . hiding in its shell.

Enough! I can't take anymore insults! Sober up, dry out! Get some professional help! Keep out of my sight! Go away!—She slams the bedroom door behind her.

Wroclaw goes to the fridge and gets himself a bottle of white wine, pours it into a coffee mug and sits down at his bureau, starts sifting through copies of photographs from the Malthrop case.

By 2am he has found the image he wants: a photograph from the now-entombed interior of Clevedane Lane, in which on the wall in the background can be clearly seen geometric lines drawn in black chalk on a white plaster wall. He sits on the living room floor against one wall with the photograph by his side and begins to try to recreate the shape. It begins like a pentagram, then a hexagon, resembles a donut, then moves towards a kind of vortex, a miasma, like a map of some insane constellation glimpsed in the farthest reaches of space.

By 3am the shape is almost complete, and Wroclaw begins to think he sees some of the lines shifting. He rubs his eyes. It's as if they're correcting themselves, taking on a life of their own. He feels enthralled, exhilarated, no longer in control.

By 4am, the wall has become soft to the touch and almost wet in places. When he prods it, it sometimes gives way and his hand vanishes into it up to his wrist.

By 5am, he has knelt and pushed, then fallen through it, laughing then coughing, choking, moving forward into blackness, too far in to withdraw. Trying to reach forward into some light he glimpses at the end of the tunnel, he is desperate for fresh air.

Disturbed and woken up by some commotion, a scuffling and muffled series of cries from the living room, Tilda gets out of bed and comes through to find only her husband's right leg left protruding from a mass of chalk lines on the living room wall.

Shrieking in fear, she dives down and grabs his foot and attempts to pull it backwards. With a final groan and great swishing of wind like the black wings of some giant raven, she feels the wall get the better of her and draw her husband through, stealing him forever.

She is left rocking back and forward on the floor, moaning and weeping like a baby, a lunatic, with only her husband's discarded shoe and sock for comfort.

Brian Lindsay and Lynn Brien compare notes at the office.
Superintendent was on the phone. Says Wroclaw's not well. Some kind of funny turn. She sounded sheepish like she knew more than she could say. I reckon it's the drink . . .

Really?

Oh yes . . . there's been signs you know. I've smelt it on his breath, Oh yes, and something else, perhaps not unconnected. She says we've to close the Malthrop case, as of now. 'Bout time too, I'd say. Complete waste of effort, load of old bollocks. The old man has got obsessed with it. Time to move on. I was just looking over the notes. Something weird in here, something Wroclaw never told us about. Did you ever see this?

Lynn takes a handwritten letter from him and unfolds it. *No, it doesn't look familiar. What is it?*

Letter to Malthrop from his dad supposedly, found inside Clevedane Lane. More like from his grand dad though. I mean, when was Kentish Town ever open fields with sheep and cows on it? Centuries ago, right?

Lynn nods her head, intrigued by the beautiful old handwriting.

Well then, have a read at that, it will make you titter. I reckon somebody was winding old Wroclaw up. Pishing in his boots and telling him it was raining. Do you think people get more naïve as they get older, Lynn?—I mean after some kind of midway point?

    Brian.

    What?

    Gonna shut up while I try and read this?

MECHAGNOSIS #09

~ *The Enigma Of Return* ~

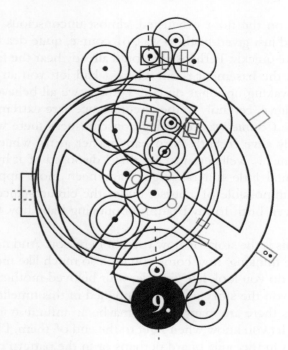

"*Praise the world to the angel, not the unsayable, you can't impress him with sumptuous feelings—in the universe where he feels things so fully you're just a novice. Show him, then, some simple thing shaped by its passage through generations that lives as a belonging near the hand, in the gaze. Tell him of Things. He'll stand more astonished than you did beside the rope-maker in Rome, or the potter by the Nile . . . "*
—Rainer Maria Rilke, from the *Duino Elegies*, #9.

Connie lay on the floor exhausted, almost unconscious. The child that she had just given birth to was, of course, quite dead. I knew I had to move quickly. Perhaps she could already hear the faint crying noise from the basement room where I had left you an hour ago. You were waking up, right on cue. Perhaps we all believe what we want to believe, certainly if the circumstances are extreme enough. By the time Connie was regaining consciousness there would be a miraculously alive recently-born baby in her arms, while the sadly deceased one . . . well, let's just say that I disposed of it hygienically. A sentimental little funeral might have been more appropriate I know, but impossible of course, under the circumstances. Connie had just given birth to my beautiful bouncing baby boy. Of course she had.

So this is the story of how you got here, son. And now I know what you're thinking: how come you look so much like me? Yes, but how much do you look like Connie, your beloved mother? You see, I'm telling you the story of what happened in this timeline, but the bad news is there are many others, maybe an infinite number, who knows? I'll let you know when I get to the end of them. I'll send you a message. On the ouija board perhaps or in the pattern of frost on an attic window, that sort of thing.

First time around, we made it to the hospital. I called an ambulance on time, I didn't pretend the line was busy, like I would do later. And at the hospital, surrounded by nurses and a doctor, our little son was born dead. And Connie was heartbroken and in shock and began what would become months of depression. She blamed herself for what was a random event, thinking it was God's vindictiveness or some other such rot, some sin being punished. I hadn't thought she had absorbed that much religious tomfoolery from her mother, but these things go in deep.

And while she lay in that place over coming days, going from bad to worse, inconsolable, she scarcely listened to me, talking to herself, running through repetitive loops of despair. Each night, the nurse finally gave her some drugs and got her off to sleep. I went home and started up that strange prototype Machine I had been building in the basement. Oh how the cogs spun, the flywheels flew, the pistons chugged, the valves hissed and spat. I dared, with the house to myself for a while, to get the Machine up to top speed, the white heat of pneumatic revolution, a blur. Shivering, shuddering, I watched light and dark, then time itself, bend inwards into my contraption.

I had tested it of course, on several hundred fruit flies and a few hapless hamsters, but never on a person. But I was desperate. I was distraught. What did I have to lose at that moment, with my child dead and my beloved wife teetering into madness? *Have to lose?* I know, I should know better. That phrase is the official tagline of destiny's worst idiots. I balanced myself on a chair, like a suicide preparing to hang himself, determined not to go back on the deal at the last minute, anxious to follow my plan through in all its magnificent recklessness. I half fell, half dived from the chair as if into a deep pond, and passed into the dark spinning vortex between the wheels of the Machine.

The Machine came slowly to a halt in a field outside the village of my childhood. Bright spring sunshine stung my eyes as I fell out of the misted door, coughing, my shirt in tatters, steam pouring off me. With a shock, I realised how surprised I was the thing had worked. Perhaps I really had expected to die. I counted all my fingers and toes, quite literally. The first hamster had come back with his innards hanging out after all, although for all I knew that just meant a sixteenth century cat had got a good swipe at him.

It took me fifteen minutes to get my legs to walk again. Then I made my way downhill, across the fields, past the mildly curious cows and sheep munching distractedly, towards the unfurling plumes of smoke from the shepherd's houses. I quickly saw I hadn't set the Machine accurately enough. For there I suddenly spotted myself: a sepia photograph come alive, playing contentedly in my little paddock, as I had remembered doing so many years ago. How strange to hear my own small voice, high-pitched and sing-song, to eavesdrop on my own childhood games, how like every other child's.

119

But it was too late. Already the spell was broken, the golden child had spotted his nemesis, the observer had changed the scene by his very presence. Dropping his little wooden sword, my younger self stared intently at me and ventured forward then back, warily. *Who ya here to see, mister?*—he piped up, furrowing his small brow, something approaching a frown, probably the nearest he could look to threatening. Spellbound, dumbstruck, I realised as I tried to speak, that I still used the same frown myself, a family characteristic no doubt, inherited perhaps, from some distant uncle or grandparent.

Your mother . . . I started to stammer, one hand in my hair, confused.

Again, curiously, I noticed he then mimicked the gesture himself, unconsciously, like the mirror of time had just smashed and my reflection and I were getting to know each other. *Not back yet . . . from the shops . . .* he pronounced nonchalantly, then turned as if to resume his game.

I looked away myself but soon found he had thought of more to say. *Do we know you, mister? Your face looks familiar. You a relative?*

Yes, yes . . . I laughed, *in a way. A distant relative. What an astute boy you are. Scott, isn't it? Young Scott Malthrop?*

Might be, he frowned again warily. *Who are you then?*

Uncle . . . I thought quickly, scanning my distant memories of family trees . . . *Uncle Peter.*

Uncle Peter's dead, Mum says. His submarine sank.

I smiled, recognising my own smug love of knowledge in my younger self, expecting it. *I held my breath and swam for it, made my way home on foot through France. Could do with a cup of char now though!*

At this the little mite's face had gone white as snow, and he turned tail and ran into the house. I helped myself to the gate latch, formulating my new purpose as I crossed the garden, calculating my options on return to the Machine.

Scott?—I called on entering the darkened house, relishing the old familiar smells: wood polish, chip fat, cigar smoke, coal, a million memories coming alive in each of them, overpowering, like a candle flame caught in a sudden wind from an open door.

But I wasn't as smart as I thought I was. Another ingrained

120

characteristic. Out of the unexpected gloom of an open doorway as I passed: a great thick hand swung and slapped into my skull, knocking me off my feet. *Who the devil d'you think you are, walking into this house, sunshine?*

With a lurch of both terror and love, in equal measure, I recognised the youthful face of my father ... who in turn recognised me not in the slightest as he grimaced threateningly, then picked me up by the lapels. I smelt drink on his breath.

Some kind of pervert, after my son? What's your business on my property? Speak up!

I struggled to speak, stammering. How could he understand, how could I hope to explain my mixture of emotions, my overwhelming joy to see him alive again, his face unwrinkled, his bent limbs straightened, his hoarse shaky voice clear and melodious again, his youthful vigour returned. But also I was trembling with fear again, remembering, anticipating, the anger and violence he was capable of.

I'm your ... your ... son ... I stammered out hopelessly, then even worse: *I'm from the future ... from a machine I built, I will build ...*

What!? The pools of his dark eyes deepened for a second, perhaps as he calculated some dates and times of previous dalliances with potential mothers, then dismissed the notion, striking me hard across the face with the back of his hand.

I was on the floor and he was kicking me. *Goddam lunatic, pervert, get out of this house, coming here scaring my son, making false accusations, after money is that what it is? Go pick on somebody richer you bastard, you gypsy, fatherless bastard, lying to foist yourselves on us! I don't know you from Adam! From flaming Adam. Am I making myself clear?*

He had me by the throat now, halfway back down the corridor, banging my head off the wall. My windpipe was constricted, one arm pinned behind my back. But with my free one, on a sudden impulse, I grabbed a table lamp and swung it into his face. I didn't expect the fabric shade to give, didn't anticipate the antiquated bulb smashing into his eyes. He was lashing out and I was lashing back now, something animal and instinctive taking over. I was fighting for my own life, at the expense of his if necessary. Indeed, I soon saw that this was exactly the bargain fate had in mind for me.

121

I was breathing fast, pumping adrenalin, fired-up with all my memories flooding back to me of how he had beaten me mercilessly as a child, for being too smart, or disrespectful, cheeky to our mother, or later: too effeminate and intellectual, not dumb and macho enough for his liking.

All this my younger self still had to look forward to . . . but my train of thought was interrupted by sobbing: the poor little mite was looking at me again now, reappeared at the far end of the hallway, watching, disbelieving at the scene I only now took in at my feet: my father in a pool of blood, unmoving. I had felled his hero.

I knelt and looked for the pulse in his neck. My head hurt, not just from the aftermath of his blows now, but from the oncoming storm, the mind-numbing implications of this unforeseen outcome. If my father was dead, prematurely, how would my future alter, if at all? What would I return to when I re-started the Machine? Struck by terror, I was instantly anxious to return, like a diver running out of oxygen, a climber on a mountain path as mist descends...

My younger version was moving closer, and knelt down now too. In strange symmetry again, we both sat, hands outstretched in tentative exploration, beseechment, towards the human being who had created us, our genesis, our fallen god. We were both crying.

I'm sorry . . . I didn't mean to . . .

Why?—we both said at once, lifting our faces. Why had I killed him he was about to ask me, why wasn't he running away now, I had been about to ask him.

You're me / I'm you . . . we both spoke over each other again, except he followed his with a question: *aren't you?*

I was impressed by his bravery and stoicism, his instant grasp of the fantastical.

Yes . . . I said, as he nodded, as if his gesture produced my words.

We both stood up simultaneously and began backing away from each other, in opposite directions, from our father's body. *Oh God . . .* again, we echoed simultaneously.

You have to go / I have to go . . . again we mirrored.

122

I turned and ran, and as if this broke some kind of temporary link, I heard his final phrase shouted after me while I was soon too breathless for any words of my own: *You have to undo this! Undo this!*

I ran from the house in panic, leapt over the fence and re-climbed the hill, through the fields, the sheep and cows running from me, startled, my alarm spreading out like ripples in the ocean of life. My heart beat in my mouth, my ears, like an infernal pendulum. As if I was a machine myself, the worst of all possible machines, one locked on accelerate without any brake pedal.

An inquisitive sheep had found a way to open the door to the cockpit of the Machine, and crows were resting on top of it, pecking fallen acorns off its upper reaches. I cried out in terror and scared off the lot of them. The beating of wings and drumming hooves merged with the tumult inside me.

I thrust open the door and collapsed onto the seat, frantically adjusting dials and levers, muttering my calculations out loud, sweat pouring off me in great rivulets that hissed when they dropped onto the still warm dashboard, the numb scientific wheels and cogs and dials, demonic machinery. *What have I done?*—I cried out to a God I had thought I no longer believed in, whom I thought I had killed. How might I have changed my own future?

The wheels were turning again. Picking up speed, the familiar rhythms shaking my body, fast, faster, soothing, the rattle becoming smoother, a hum, a blur. The glass was misting. The world was gone. My head was thrown back. My bones shook, jolted, were pushed beyond substance, beyond matter into light. Silence. Sleep. Infinity. All time. No time.

Morning. I was waking somewhere. Light, silence. The world was back. My arm flailed out, as the fetid atmosphere of my own sweat and breath choked me. I found the door release and rolled out sideways, falling, coughing into the blinding light, on my knees, into God knows what.

I had passed out again. Maybe only minutes later, or maybe hours. I was on my side on the floor, looking at my familiar basement room again, my workshop, thank Christ. I slowly dragged myself up, limbs aching, head hungover, eyes blurry. I looked around the room for clues, changes. I staggered out of the room and made my way up the stairs, heart breaking with remorse and trepidation, love and fear.

And then like the light of mercy, each note falling as rays of hope, I heard Connie's voice singing . . . singing. Gently, sweetly. Tears welled up in my eyes. I opened the kitchen door and saw her there at the stove, the most beautiful and welcome sight that has ever met human eyes. I crossed the floor and she spun around and we embraced. *Oh you silly thing, you . . .* she laughed as we kissed and she touched my face, -*What's the matter with you now?*

Have I been gone long?—I asked, hugging her tightly again, thanking every God on Mount Olympus for her.

No, just ten minutes, she said, *I was just about to come down and fetch you . . .*

Why? I laughed nervously.

Because dinner's ready, silly . . . she said, turning to attend to the bubbling pot.

I looked down at her stomach and something hit me. *Connie, are you pregnant?*

Not yet, sweet. Not as far as I know, must just be looking tubby today. I thought you said you liked this dress, you said it was . . .

No, no, I just wondered . . .

We'll keep trying, dear. Doctor said it might take a few months.

I looked at the calendar on the wall. What month is this, Conn?

April, silly. You been inhaling engine fumes again down there, lost the plot? What is it you do down there anyway? Can't you sell any of those weird machines? Get an agent and art gallery to exhibit them or something. Make us some money?

I was exactly two years further back in time. My mind reeled with a new excitement. *Can I just go and switch my lathe off, honey?— And I think I left a drill plugged in. I'll be back up in a second . . .*

I backed away and ran down the stairs then started the Machine up again, jotting down hand calculations of years and days. But then something happened that I should have foreseen. Why did it catch me so much by surprise? Startled perhaps by the sounds I was making, a figure emerged from the hall storeroom, face splashed with engine oil and dust, and locked eyes with me. We both froze, ten feet apart. *Oh Fuck,* I said.

He laughed. *Ahhh . . . don't worry, I won't get in your way,* he said calmly, wiping his hands with a towel, but keeping a close eye on me all the time. *I know what you're up to, but don't fret, it all works out . . .*

Tentatively, I began to turn away, to resume my work, then stopped. *"Works" out? Future tense? You mean . . . .?*

Yes, he nodded, *but better not to ask, cross-contamination and all that. Just get back in there and get on with it. I'll stay out your way.*

But shouldn't you know less than me, not more?

No, or then you'd have to have a memory of this meeting, wouldn't you? Look, don't ask, don't try to understand. You'll get here soon enough. Now . . . go!

I finished off my calculations and climbed back into the Machine, confused, but somehow trusting, exhilarated, terrified. He even waved me goodbye.

This time a cow had positioned herself unluckily: I found her sliced in half by the rear-end of the Machine, and still twitching. Regretful, I knelt and broke her neck. The crows were gathering on the tree overhead, smelling blood. I returned to the house and found it empty this time. I rapped on the windows. I called on a few neighbours. Gone to the hospital they said, her first child expected, they smiled warmly, convinced by my visiting relative story, swayed by the family resemblance. So far so good.

I waited until nightfall, hiding in the woods behind the house, waiting to hear the car returning, the lights going on and yes . . . the sounds of a baby crying, a newborn, my own younger self. So near so far.

What was I contemplating? The risks were enormous, the crime required: a heinous one. If I died, I died. But if the baby died, I died again also, probably. Was that how it would work? My recent encounter in the basement had suggested that there was a hint of infinity about all this, of multiplication, parallelism. Anything seemed possible, morality seemed absent. Or so I thought.

At three in the morning, I rose from my hiding place and made my way carefully, silently, through the hedge, and the fence, into the garden. I moved from window to window on tip-toe,

125

peering in. There they were at last, the three of them, asleep, unknowing. A young family, cherished image of innocence and hope, bathed in moonlight. And if any of them had woken at that moment what would they have made of me?—How could they conceive of what and why and how I was?—What I was doing here? Of course, they would scream.

I was amazed at my own ill-preparedness. I couldn't go through with it. I made excuses for myself as I hovered, vacillated, cogitated, agonised. I needed chloroform. Of course I did. And I had some back at my workshop, which I had used successfully on hamsters and stray cats. It was reason enough. It bought me time. I withdrew.

The Machine again. Travel. Time. Pain. This time as I returned to the basement I resolved to be quick about it, hunting around in my cupboards to find the right drugs. I wouldn't even risk going up to see Connie. Then I heard a voice above calling out: *Is there anybody there?—We're calling the police!*

I recognised its tone. I would have laughed at its mock forcefulness were I not so startled. As the footsteps came down the stairs I almost instinctively threw open the door and put my foot out on the mud, before thinking better of it, coming back in and hiding in the cupboard. In he came with a torch and a baseball bat, looking around himself feverishly, a frightened animal. Even as he did, the memory suddenly came back to me of the break-in I thought I had thwarted shortly after Connie and I had first moved in. My God, I was fooling myself now, quite literally. Somehow this version, unlike that other smart-arse, had no knowledge of what would happen in the future. He was an earlier version of me, blissfully ignorant, now carefully re-bolting his door and resolving to purchase a burglar alarm.

Again, I almost laughed or cried out in exultation to realise that some kind of rule, some kind of invisible force field of causality was protecting me now. Whatever I did, I already knew that the man out there with his baseball bat would not discover me, would go back upstairs unaware of my presence. But then also on reflection I realised, somehow even if I decided to cry out and try to give myself away, yes, somehow something would intervene and prevent that also. I could no more change this scenario than

I could make myself jump off a cliff, that's to say: it might be possible, but only after a lot of practice and rehearsal to overcome my own built-in fail-safes, my self-preservation instincts, real physical forces in my body.

There was no time to think it all through properly. Indeed, perhaps it was ultimately incomprehensible, but right there and then I knew, or should I say I felt, what consciousness really is, and it's not what we take it for most of the time. We are on rails, and freewill is an illusion. If our innermost feelings are real, it is only in so far as they exist outside of time itself.

Once he was gone, I set the Machine going again, with a minor adjustment. More pain and dislocation, but I was starting to get used to the side-effects. I found myself weeks, perhaps a few months later than before, and re-found that nocturnal scene. The baby, my little self in waiting, had been decanted to another room, into a cot. Sleeping soundly. Nothing could be more perfect. Again that feeling of fate, of pre-destination. Some things are too easy, *too possible* for us not to yield to them, as if actions, events, are crystallisations, currents born of some hidden magnetism just below the surface of life, a landscape made long ago, sculpted by some dark other.

I turned the front door handle. Of course it wasn't locked, we never locked it back then, not even at night. It was a more innocent world, a less urban one. Another door opened and then I was crossing the room to look at my little treasure. A floorboard creaked a little, and I hung back then moved sideways, holding my breath. There I was. He slept. His innocent little face, nose and mouth turned up to take in all that was coming to him. I wet the rag from the bottle of chloroform then held it carefully under his nose, listening to his breathing, trying to put my own on hold.

Then disaster, I heard a bed heaving, other floorboards creaking, someone getting up in the next room. Utterly panicked, I clutched my bottle and rushed over to a wardrobe, hiding behind the coats inside and peering out through the gap between the doors. This was getting to be a habit.

My mother walked in, in her nightdress, carrying a bedside lantern, kneeling lovingly to survey her sleeping son. I watched her intently, my heart thumping so loud in my ears I was sure she must

127

be hearing it too. She stroked his face then seemed satisfied, pacified and turned to go. Then she halted. She had noticed something, she tilted her head, bent down. Oh no. Liquid. Drops of chloroform had landed on the cot, on the floor.

Something inside me, to even my own surprise, swung into action, with utter urgency and conviction. I lunged from the cupboard and grabbed her from behind, held her in a headlock with one arm, and put a massive dose of chloroform under her nose with the other.

Her body went limp, and I lowered her carefully to the floor. Her nightdress fell open and her long black hair fell across her face in the moonlight. I looked down at her neck, her knees, her ankles, and the fine youthful curves of everything that went on in between. God, no. I took a hard-on. I wanted to scream. It was simple biology, but at that moment it seemed like the worst of all possible condemnations of me, from God himself perhaps. This, as Americans say, was messed up. There I was feeling achingly horny, staring at my own helpless mother. Freud was right, the bastard. I even considered . . . No I couldn't think straight. This was my mother, and when she awoke she would find her child gone and be utterly panicked and distraught, grief-stricken, driven half-mad for the rest of her life. How could I do this to her?

To my relief now I saw my erection was subsiding. Maybe if I was truly humane I would have killed her. I looked around the room and saw a thick rope curtain-pull by the window . . . something I remembered I had later played with as a child. I had a knife in my pocket. I could strangle her with that cord I thought for a moment, end her life in her sleep so she never had to wake and endure the pain of losing her child, of losing me. But how would God, if he existed, judge me for such a crime? How would I judge myself?

But I had less abstract dilemmas than that to face. How could I be sure of what timeline I was in? It came back to me suddenly that my mother had once mentioned a miscarriage, losing a child before I came along. What if that had been a euphemism? In which case, if I was yet to be conceived, then by killing her would I instantly cease to exist? Or worse still perhaps if I were to . . . oh no, again my eyes wandered onto her exposed upper thigh. If I were to . . . then I would be my own . . . . or my little brother would be . . . oh God, no, the possibilities were endless and monstrous.

As if to save me from all this delay, I heard a bedspring shift in the other room, my father turning in his sleep. I did the only thing I could. I grabbed the baby, my own tiny sleeping self, wrapped him snugly in one of his own favourite blankets and fled from the house, running faster and faster uphill towards the waiting Machine, listening all the time for some ominous sound from behind me, some awful cry of anger or vengeance from my father, some sign that a terrible pursuit had begun. But it never came.

Once, I tripped on a rock and I rolled over like a parachutist, absorbing the blow into my rolling body, desperate to keep the baby unharmed in my arms. If I injured or killed him inadvertently, would I instantly be wounded or killed myself? It seemed too far-fetched. We were both very much flesh and blood it seemed, just taken from different places in time, no different from clones or twins. But even this terrible loss I had just inflicted on my mother, would this alter the future I was about to return to? Would Connie even recognise me, or never have known me?—not even be there? Would a million tiny differences, a cascade of divergent causality, have forged an entirely different world, where everyone spoke Esperanto and drove Sinclair C5's?

The final adjustment took some fine-tuning, but I arrived back exactly where I wanted to be, a few hours before Connie went into labour. My little baby self was waking up and I ran around getting some milk for him, breaking into the baby-food packs Connie and I had stored in preparation in the basement freezers. And that meant . . . of course it did . . . the same packaging . . . maybe the world hadn't changed at all? So far so good, I rocked little baby-me in my arms and walked around the basement rooms and cupboards, finding no other versions of myself hiding, half-thinking they might have come in handy this time around to help look after the baby and change his nappies while I went up to see Connie.

After that, it all happened pretty much like I've told you already, son. I delayed calling the ambulance so that your mother would give birth at home, then I swapped the dead child for you. You're not my son. You're me. Identical, but with a different childhood now, the one we gave you. And quite a lot better one,

129

though I say so myself. I never beat you like our father did. How could I, when I understood your every action and every motive, even before you did?

Your mother never knew, and I never told her before she died last year, although I had plenty of opportunity. How would she ever have believed it? And if you don't, then feel free to compare our DNA or fingerprints. You'll get some funny looks at the lab.

I'll never forget Connie's delight when she first sat up and marvelled at you, took you in her exhausted arms and wept tears of joy over your perfection. You cried too, screamed in fact, like all babies do, probably asking for your real mother back, but nobody ever knows or understands what a baby is really saying or asking for, do they? Maybe that's just as well or we'd hear all their complaints about their previous incarnations, the dead ancestors they thought they were just a moment before they woke up and found life starting all over again. Whatever they see and say, I have no doubt at all that it is terrifying. They certainly succeed in conveying that much.

Meanwhile somewhere else in time, in some other version of time, I knew my mother wept and goes on weeping eternally for the loss of me -For how I so cruelly stole the child I was from her one night, leaving her bereft forever. But that just sounds like growing up and leaving home, doesn't it? The prodigal son. Oh Mother, Mother, when will I ever return to you to beg forgiveness for this and all other things? Sometime, soon enough, perhaps we all face that reunion.

I phoned the doctor again, and the ambulance, this time expecting to get through. But the line was dead. That was odd. I tried not to show my concern, and changed the sheets and tried to make Connie comfortable. As she sat up and delighted in the child I had given her, I walked away for a minute to get some fresh air and look out on the world I had got back, returned to, unscathed after all my tribulations. I wanted to rejoice in it, celebrate that nothing had changed. It was night time, late summer. I threw open the front door expecting to breathe in the deep nocturnal air, to touch the leaves, hear the late murmurings of traffic.

But I looked down from the threshold and saw that there

was no path anymore, no garden, no street, no city. I looked up and instead of night sky I saw only blackness, the infinite blankness of empty space, above and below. Then gradually, the harder and closer I looked I saw that instead of stars there were eyes, in their innumerable trillions, staring back at me, watchful, judgemental, expectant.

The chill wind of eternity blew over me and shivered through my soul.

MECHAGNOSIS #10

~ *Forgiving Everything* ~

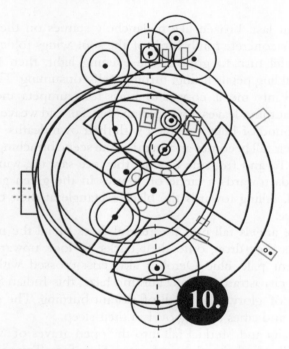

10.

"That someday at the close of this fierce vision I might sing praise and jubilation to assenting angels. That the heart's clear-striking hammers might not falter from landing on slack or doubtful or snapping strings . . . "
—Rainer Maria Rilke, from the *Duino Elegies*, #10.

Autumn at last. Frozen like melancholy statues on the roof of Malthrop's concrete tomb, birds of the soul, wings folded: Seralta and Merkiel turn to gold in the evening light, then fire, then rose. Crinkling petals lifting, turning, self-consuming. They burn, burnished into metal, copper or brass for trumpets and shields. They are autumn leaves now, folding, they fall and weave the wind like the sound of bells, pregnant with their own deaths.

Their fall becomes another day, the scene bleaching through this one. To and fro, side to side, they see-saw the wind, falling downwards towards a circle of figures in the green grass of a graveyard, falling towards the black rectangle at their centre: an open grave.

The angels fall past the tearful faces of all the mourners, turning as they drop, onto their backs, to look upwards at the magnificent pale blue October sky, criss-crossed with vapour trails and cirrostratus, smoky autumn haze, this Indian Summer's last blaze of glory. The smell of distant burning. The sound of eyelashes and cities turning over in their sleep.

Seralta and Merkiel fall into the open graves of Mitch and Melanie Cheswick, brother and sister. They fuse. Time reaches its still point, a singularity, light and sound begin to groan to a halt, sounds of protestation like cosmic brakes thrown on, shuddering of air, shattering of reality like a mirror struck, breaking soundlessly. The fragments fall down in slow motion. The smallest movement of fingers or lips slows and intensifies to a deafening roaring and tearing. The slightest word on the tongue deepens to a low growl, incomprehensible, threatening.

Wroclaw sits up on the floor of No.15a Clevedane Lane and finds himself facing Scott Malthrop at last. *You . . .* he says. Malthrop stands in front of three storeys of machinery, the shapes and intersections of cogs now strangely familiar to Wroclaw after months of studying the scale model. Malthrop's face and overalls are stained with oil, like some common everyday mechanic, roadside engineer, poised beside a flying machine or steam engine.

To Wroclaw's amazement, Malthrop's expression changes into one of even greater awe than his own. He puts down his spanner and kneels devoutly in front of Wroclaw. *You've come at last. I've waited for so long. For centuries it seems . . .*

Who are you? Wroclaw gasps, backing away, not even sure anymore what he means by such a question.

I wish I knew, Malthrop says gently, then begins to weep. *I hoped you might give me the answer. Please . . .* He reaches out his hands towards him imploringly, on his knees, as Wroclaw recoils. *Please, Father. Tell me who I am. I did all this for you . . . to gain your attention . . . to impress you. To hold up a mirror and ask you who I was. So who are we? Won't you tell me what we are?*

Father?—Wroclaw asks, shaking, confused. *You think I'm your . . . ?*

Malthrop breaks down at this and sobs uncontrollably. *Don't disown me now, not now, after all this time. You created me. All I ever wanted was to be accepted, to be understood. Not this constant humiliation called life, this uncertainty and loneliness . . . oh God . . . I've been so alone for so long . . . hold me, please . . .*

Reluctantly, shivering, backed into a corner, Wroclaw finds himself embracing Malthrop who sobs and shakes against him saying: *don't you know me?*

When Malthrop tries to kiss his cheek, something stirs in Wroclaw, some strange animal revulsion and anger, hatred of his smell, his presumptuous intimacy. *I know evil . . .* he answers and puts his hands around his throat. Malthrop goes on weeping as he begins to choke, still trying to say over and over again: *Father, Father . . .*

Another change comes, the pain, the disappointment, provokes anger in Malthrop, the primal urge to survive, to resist attack. He punches against Wroclaw, lashes out, stands up, and the two men struggle and fight, throwing each other around the room, their words degenerating into animal cries.

Encased in concrete, lost somewhere outside of time, their shouts go unheard, their battle rages towards infinity, like the

135

childhood memory of thunder and lightning on a summer day, or the winds of a winter storm at night, hid from beneath grey blankets.

Something happens. The Machinery finally groans and quakes and grinds to a complete halt, some tiny flaw perhaps, or wear and tear, a grain of sand or rice has caught in a wheel of time and stopped the universe. God pauses at last and listens, awakened, moved by our cries.

From their funeral, their burials, Mitch and Melanie move backwards, their coffins carrying them to the pathology lab then back to the crime scene, back to their last moments with Malthrop. Instead of killing them and dismembering and dissolving them, he recreates them out of bone and sinew and blood. He builds these two most wonderful of his creations and sends them both back out into the world with his love, waving them goodbye warmly, like a proud and tearful mother.

He meets them again on various occasions. The reunions are emotional, particularly with Melanie, his favourite. He even has to take her clothes off and examine her sometimes, to make sure she is still working properly. But even with her in the end these meetings grow less frequent, colder, more formal.

Finally, there comes one sad occasion in a wooden summerhouse in the rain when they say their last words to each other, parting forever, and her eyes become stranger's eyes, glassy, impersonal, uncaring, cold as she walks away backwards. They are strangers now forever from this moment onwards, passing each other in the street, never saying hello, never even remembering each other. This is the saddest of human tragedies: to forget.

But this is Malthrop's gift to the angels. His Machine has brought them down into human bodies and let them taste the nectar of earthly longing. He lets them grow young again in the light of dead summers. On the beach of memory they will run side by side into the sun, towards the ever-receding, glittering waves.

Face to face, fighting, struggling, Wroclaw and Malthrop become one, blur, merge, re-emerge on the other side of each other, transfigured, facing in opposite directions.

Malthrop steps backwards out of the chalk lines on Wroclaw's living room wall and rewinds Wroclaw's evening, his life, neatly throwing up all that alcohol into glasses and handing it all over to the very polite barman who kindly disposes of it hygienically and arranges for it to all be transported away to be treated in complex metal vats and stills to turn it all back into beautiful fields of barley swaying in the sun.

Moving backwards, he grows to love Tilda's face and body and all those kind patient words she sucks out of the air in front of him, always taking arguments away. Leaving him feeling better and better, more youthful by the minute. He is horrified when he finds himself in bed with another woman and quickly disposes of her, getting all the alcohol out of her, getting her out of his life. Tilda and him get closer and closer after that, younger and happier until he wakes up to find her in a wedding dress one day, and knows what's coming next, delighted.

They talk about having children after the ceremony, but as the weeks and months and years go by he sees that something even better is on the cards: they're going to become them.

Wroclaw steps into the Machine. Gleaming, humming with power, beautifully maintained, this is his prize. He looks at it all and understands at last all the parts that were wrong, the little flaws he missed, the things he could so easily have fixed if only he'd thought hard enough before. He sees the total picture now, the supreme harmony. Indeed, its creator, Malthrop, must have been God.

Climbing into the cockpit, donning his goggles, he feels a pang of loneliness for a moment for Malthrop. How sad that he is gone,—that he has lost him forever, the sublime architect, and that all he has left to know and remember him by is this, his magnificent Machine.

Is it enough? Would it be better to have Malthrop with him, at his shoulder, to explain its workings, to share in his joy? Or is the Machine so perfect that Malthrop himself, his very essence, is contained and expressed in its every movement?

But Malthrop just seemed like a man, face to face. No more or less interesting, boring or flawed and disappointing than any of the rest of them. There were even awkward silences in their conversation. Imagine.

But here inside his Machine, this is the real and only way to know Malthrop totally, to become him, to understand his dreams and dream them for him, to take them further now and next, beyond where even he had gone or thought before.

The Machine was Malthrop, his body only a vessel, temporary, surplus, discarded, a dried husk, his mission accomplished.

Wroclaw turns the dials and adjusts the levers, tightens the straps. He sets a course for Malthrop's childhood. He has a hunch that this time around things will be different, that every cycle of the Machine produces different results.

He hits the Starter switch and hears the whirring of actuators and pumps, the beautiful music of fuel and power, sublime organisation and progress. For a moment it sounds like Bach, or angels singing. He smiles.

When I said close the Malthrop case, I didn't mean destroy it, Lynn.

What are you talking about, Brian?—Lynn furrows her brow, cradling her paper coffee cup by the fax machine. Blades of morning sunlight criss-cross the grey carpet from the dusty blinds on the high Georgian-wired windows, the traffic groaning faintly through an open window like a slumbering brontosaurus, the manifest sigh of paper trays and pin boards and shirts and ties.

The superintendent just asked to see it, and here it is, I go get it and open it up and there's nothing in it. How can that be? April Fool's Day? You trying to convince me I'm the next drunken madman around here? Lynn sees Brian is genuinely angry and confused, but also speaking too loudly, playing to the gallery.

Oh . . . .. tut tut tut. Lynn laments his disrespectful remark, but can tell from the general murmur across the office that this is just a foretaste of things to come. History written by the victors. The young dancing on the ashes of their parents, as some old poet said somewhere. *Must be some mistake, I've not been near it. Have you changed the locks yet? Maybe old Rock Arse himself has been in and blagged it . . .*

Another murmur across the room from her various half-listening colleagues. Lynn enjoys the response but is dismayed to see herself stooping to the same level.

In her lunch break, when Brian is safely out of the way, Lynn lies back in her chair and takes a small notebook from her pocket, one saved from Wroclaw's file: Melanie Cheswick's last diary. She looks around to check that nobody's spying over her shoulder, then reads it, touched by its hope and innocence. When she reaches the end, she wipes a tear from her eye.

Tuesday 16th March.

The neighbours are making some bloody racket tonight, damn student party I suppose, and me with work tomorrow. I met this sweet boy last week. Scott Malthrop. I say boy, but actually he's eight years older than me. God, I hope that's not too much is it? He doesn't look that old. In fact (but why would he be lying?) he looks the same age as me, early twenties. He's very kind and clever, in a shy sort of way, which is quite endearing actually. He says he's a jeweller, his father's business. He's probably rich but not so you'd notice. Dresses very demurely, but not shabbily you understand. Just not the showy type, that's all.

He is so thoughtful. Or soulful, maybe that's the word. We've gone for some long walks together and he has so many ideas and theories about life. He's so intrigued to learn about me. You wouldn't believe the amount of detail he remembers. He's like a sponge. I never knew I was so fascinating!

Saturday 3rd April.

Been seeing Scott again. Went to the pictures then another long walk. Lovely spring evening, be summer soon. I couldn't believe it, turns out he lost his mother too, a tragic accident, something in

139

the home, he wouldn't be specific, obviously an upsetting memory. He's such a sensitive guy. Then I told him about what happened to my mum and dad. How Mitch is all I've got left. It was all very moving. We seem to have such an empathy when we're together. He says his dad is quite old and infirm now, suspected Alzheimer's, confined to a wheelchair. That explains why Scott isn't able to get out much. He seems to dote over his father, and the old guy sounds pretty difficult at times. My heart goes out to him, he's such a saint.

Friday 16th April.

Scott's so clever. Somebody's car had broken down in the street today and he just went over and repaired it on the spot. Repaired it! The guy drove it off five minutes later, and it wasn't a simple repair. I thought he was just going to help him push it off the main road but no. I asked him afterwards if he had trained as a mechanic and he just laughed. "Grey fingers", he calls it. An affinity with all machines. He promised to build me a watch today. From scratch, from materials in his workshop, says his watches are all one-offs. I'm so excited, I hope he means it. I can't wait.

Sunday 18th April.

He wasn't joking. He gave me the watch today, just two days later, with my initials engraved inside it. It's full of tiny cogs and things, amazing little mechanisms, all exposed and tricky and intricate. It's like a mechanical flower or something. I'm so honoured. This guy's amazing. So talented and completely different. He's not like a person, he's like a whole city to himself, if you know what I mean. I'd love to see his workshop and maybe meet his dad, even though he does sound a bit scary.

Wednesday 19th May.

Went to the seaside today with Scott. What a guy. Some kids were flying remote controlled planes and he showed one how to adapt its wings to improve uplift. Then he tied black paper strips to it to make it look like it had feathers, then sent it up so that a flock of crows started checking it out and chasing it off like they thought it was a rival. He sellotaped my mobile phone to it then downloaded the pictures from it afterwards in a hi-fi shop, looking down on the town like it was a postage stamp. It was crazy. The children all thought he was some kind of magician. Then on the way home the bus hit a pigeon and he made the driver stop while he got out. I had to follow him and the bus just went off without us. He sat on the pavement for ten minutes cradling the bird while it died, weeping. The guy is weird, but somehow he moves me more than I can say . . . . or explain.

Thursday 3ʳᵈ June.

Scott's getting stranger. Or am I only getting to know him a bit better? I asked again to meet his father and see his workshop and he went quiet then got angry. I'd never seen him like that before. I suppose that was our first fight. Of course everyone says those are normal, but he scared me a bit. I reckon he's still traumatised by his mother's death. And by caring for his father. I know how terrible it is to watch someone you love slowly fall apart like that.

Monday 14ᵗʰ June.

I shouldn't have done this. But I was curious. Well, OK. Nosey, I suppose you'd call it. No. If you're having a relationship with someone you have the right to know certain things, don't you? I got Parcel Express to send a courier round to call at Scott Malthrop's address and deliver a jewellery catalogue and ask for the signature of his father. I phoned them up afterwards and know what they said? Apparently Scott told them his father had been dead five years. Now how weird is that? Why would someone say or do a thing like that? This is getting too freaky.

Sunday 20th June.

Really excited. Just heading out to meet Scott. After our last fight he's agreed to take me home to meet his dad after all, and show me his workshop. Says he'll explain everything. Mitch says he doesn't like the look of Scott much, but what does he know? I know we're close, but I'm not his mother, am I? He has to let me have my own life. He has Carrie after all, the snooty bitch, and I don't say anything about her, do I? Not to his face anyway. I think this will be a watershed tonight, well, make or break anyway, after which mine and Scott's relationship can only grow and get stronger. A bird has just landed on the windowsill with a broken wing . . .

Carrie Crawford and Tilda Wroclaw sit together on a summer afternoon on the balcony of Carrie's apartment overlooking the Regent's Canal, sunbathing. Brightly-painted barges nudge the quayside below, and distant sounds of traffic, markets and outdoor dining, flicker up to their ears through the languid air.

Tilda nearly asks Carrie how she can afford such a place until she remembers about the insurance payout for Mitch's death then bites her lip. She rebukes herself for the disreputable thought that her husband's coma has somehow robbed her of such compensation, albeit only financial.

It is surprising that Tilda and Carrie haven't met sooner, given the hospital visiting hours, and surprising they haven't tried to phone each other. But more surprising still that they have found each other to be almost instant friends rather than the suspicious rivals at least one of them might have expected.

Nonetheless, glass of Bacardi and ice in hand, feet up, Tilda finally feels compelled and relaxed enough to ask the inevitable question, suddenly and without any pre-amble: *So did you sleep with him, Carrie? I don't mind* . . .

But her sentence is cut off by Carrie's laughter and a spray of lemonade from her mouth all over the glass balustrade. *You're joking . . . You think . . . !?*

Tilda shrugs, smiling, nearly laughing herself now. It's in

poor taste, but somehow a relief to both women after the months of visiting Wroclaw's unmoving form propped up in bed, his eyes closed, his brain unresponsive even to tapes of his beloved Bach.

We were friends . . . sorry, forgive me, shouldn't use the past tense. We were good friends, Tilda, I enjoyed our conversations, but heavens, I never thought of him like . . . you know . . . the age difference.

A cloud crosses the sun and Tilda unexpectedly feels herself close to tears for a minute. *I think I . . . I almost wish . . . you had, you know.*

W-what?—Carrie marvels, her hand running through her long blonde hair, pushing up her dark glasses.

He's never waking up again, let's face it, Carrie. I think we both know that.

Carrie nods her head and sniffs, bringing her dark glasses back down again.

I almost wish he'd enjoyed himself more, with me, with anyone.

Carrie reaches out a hand and Tilda does not refuse it, the young giving comfort to the old. *Don't beat yourself up. Everyone does it.*

But where is he? That's what I keep asking myself. If he's not dead, then where is he?

Well, Carrie sighs, *you saw him today, all we can say for sure I think is that he is in some other reality.*

A pair of swans flap majestically by and land spectacularly on the canal water below, applauded by a few tourists in beer gardens. *You know he thought Malthrop's machine was some kind of time-travelling device? I've still got a scale model of it he had made, in my living room. I think he'd lost his mind by then.*

Carrie nods. *Yes, obsession doesn't really cover it, does it?*

You know I found him with his head halfway through a wall? He'd dug a hole right through one of our plasterboard walls, looking for a time portal or something ridiculous . . .

The poor dear . . . Carrie shakes her head.

Carrie? I meant to say . . . Tilda rouses herself, shifting in her chair, *I'm actually quite surprised you bought an apartment like this, I mean so close to the canal, so close to where you last saw Mitch. I would have expected you to want to move away. That's what most people do after a . . . a death.*

I don't know . . . Carrie sighs. *Somehow I feel closer to Mitch here, and to . . . your husband.* She casts Tilda a glance, *-if you don't mind me saying that. Maybe some part of me wants to believe all that time travel nonsense . . . maybe some part of me expects Mitch to come walking down that towpath again, magically rejuvenated from his own past. I'm haunted I suppose you'd call it. We're a generation of disbelievers you know . . . disbelievers of everything, even the moon landings, but sometimes I think that deep inside us all there's a residual faith still left over. It doesn't even know what it wants anymore, but it's there and we can't shake it off.*

Should we? It gets us out our beds every morning, doesn't it?

Yes, Carrie laughs, raising her drink, *I suppose it does. Faith in the unknown, faith in our own stupidity, faith that we don't yet know it all.*

I'll drink to that, Tilda whispers, and smiles.

As Tilda parts from Carrie later that afternoon they promise to stay in touch. They probably even mean it. On her way home Tilda decides to walk through the open-air markets and, for reasons not entirely apparent to herself, buys a bag of lemons.